"You know why I have to keep Dina sweet."

Scott's voice was harsh, and Kate knew he was controlling his temper with an effort. "She's no nickel-and-dime investment. If she delays the movie with a tantrum it could be very costly."

"So to keep her happy, you're willing to prostitute yourself?"

"What's that supposed to mean?"

"Don't tell me you didn't go home with her last night."

"Why, you . . . ." Words failed him and he pushed her away violently. "You've got the mind of a sewer rat!"

"And you've got the morals of one!" Kate snapped. "So let's stop pretending!"

"Why should I pretend with you?" he asked, and the room was suddenly very quiet. "You mean nothing to me, Kate. I don't have to account to you."

Man of Gold

Kay Clifford

Harlequin Books

TORONTO • NEW YORK • LONDON
AMSTERDAM • PARIS • SYDNEY • HAMBURG
STOCKHOLM • ATHENS • TOKYO • MILAN

Original hardcover edition published in 1983
by Mills & Boon Limited
under the title *Heart of Gold*
ISBN 0-373-02611-0

Harlequin Romance first edition April 1984

To
'the boys' — Paul, Neil and Andrew
with all my love

CHAPTER ONE

A LULL in the morning rush hour traffic set Kate Ashton darting across the Embankment. Breathless, she passed through the revolving doors at the staff entrance to Blakes and dived into the ancient cage lift just as the attendant was about to clang the gate shut.

The last of the grand hotels in London that was still family owned and operated, Blakes' detractors referred to it as an architectural monstrosity, best consigned to rubble and rebuilt as a marble and glass edifice more in keeping with its showcase setting overlooking the Thames. But to its admirers and loyal clientele, the idea of any change was sacrilege. Which was why its red brick and Portland stone façade, ornate interior and impeccable service—despite present-day staff difficulties—remained essentially the same as the day it had opened in the last year of Queen Victoria's reign.

As the lift creaked its way upwards Kate, as always, reflected on her good luck that she should be working there. And not just as an ordinary secretary either, but as personal assistant to Roger Blake, with duties that included public relations and a salary and perks that were the envy of all her friends. How, fresh from college, she had managed to convince the elderly and ultra-conservative owner that she was capable of replacing the woman who had been his right hand for more than thirty-five years, she did not know. Perhaps her background as the daughter of a hotelier had favoured her as much as an excellent curriculum vitae, that included a course in Hotel Administration—from which she had graduated with honours—and first-class secretarial qualifications. But whatever, she had fitted into the vacant slot like a newly minted penny, and proved his faith in her to be fully justified by coping not only with her own varied tasks, but also with the many queries which, unable to be answered by other departments, were invariably shunted up to her office for sorting out. Much of the information required was not her job to deal with, but she found it quicker to do it than refer it back to the people concerned, as her predecessor had done. Roger Blake accused her of being a workaholic, but had shown his approval for her endeavours by raising her salary and assigning her a secretary of her own to relieve her of some of the more routine chores.

At first Kate had worried that Janet Williams, who had been at Blakes all her working life and had aspired to her own position, would not take kindly to being told what to do by a young, inexperienced girl. But within a week she had learned that the older woman had no time to waste on envy, and was only concerned with doing her job well. It was an arrangement that had worked ideally for more than two years, and though this was Kate's first day back at work after a three-week holiday in Italy, she had every confidence that her secretary had coped admirably during her absence.

'No need to ask if you enjoyed yourself—you look fabulous!' The plump grey-haired widow looked up from her typewriter, as Kate entered the office.

Kate smiled, her even white teeth made even more dazzling by the tan she had acquired round the pool in Capri.

'If it weren't for a sore bottom I'd feel fabulous too!' she said. 'It's about time Italian men learned to keep their hands to themselves!'

'When I'm around they always do!' Janet Williams chuckled.

Kate hung her blazer on the coat stand and settled in the cream leather chair behind her desk, its capacious width emphasising her slightness. 'How has Mr Blake been treating you?' she asked.

'Impatiently—but then he's had a lot on his mind.'

'Such as?'

For answer, the woman placed a couple of newspapers on the desk, both open at the financial page.

Kate stared at the large black headlines with shock. She couldn't believe it. Blakes had been sold, totally and completely! Even worse, the buyer was Midas International, an American hotel conglomerate.

'Blakes is the last link in my chain,' Scott Jeffreys, the man behind Midas, was quoted as saying. 'I now own a hotel in every major capital city of the Western world— Peking, here I come!'

When he had been asked if he intended to impose Midas's standard of uniformity on Blakes, his reply had been typical of the man.

'If by uniformity you mean profitability, then the answer is yes. I am in business to make money, not a philanthropist with an urge to preserve ancient monuments.'

It was this latter statement which chilled Kate most. 'That means the end of Blakes as we know it,' she commented, as she slowly absorbed the unpleasant news. 'I wonder how it will affect us?'

'You'll have to ask Mr Blake about that,' Mrs Williams replied. 'He told me to send you up as soon as you arrived. He's slept here since the negotiations began.'

Although Roger Blake lived in the stockbroker belt in Weybridge, just outside London, he kept one of the penthouse suites for his own use and often stayed there when working late or spending an evening in town with his wife. It had been furnished by his grandfather, who had built the hotel, only the curtains and carpets had ever been changed, and Kate never entered the suite without the feeling of being transported back in time.

It was walnut-panelled; an ornately carved desk and fireplace dominated the vast, high-ceilinged study, so that even the distinguished figure of the hotel's proprietor merged into insignificance beside them.

Of medium height, he was as usual immaculately turned out, in black morning suit, complete with winged collar and cravat. At seventy, his face was heavily seamed, and though his eyes had lost some of their brightness, they could still sparkle at a pair of slim ankles and a pretty face.

'Glad to have you back,' he greeted her warmly. 'Janet did her best, but she's not a patch on you.'

Kate acknowledged the compliment with a smile. 'It appears she's had quite a bit to contend with while I've been away enjoying myself.'

'You mean the takeover? No doubt you were surprised.'

'It was rather sudden,' she ventured. Though she was well aware that the hotel's financial position had been far from healthy, Blakes was, like *The Times*, something of a national institution, and one she had never envisaged disappearing from the London scene.

'It's been in my mind for a long while,' Roger Blake said. 'As you know, we've been losing money for years, and frankly I can't afford to go on financing those losses. If I had had a son, perhaps I would have soldiered on, but with three daughters . . .' He sighed heavily. 'Scott Jeffreys' offer came out of the blue the day after you went on holiday. I had to make up my mind quickly, because Midas had their eyes on another hotel in London as well. Apparently their team of bloodhounds have been sniffing around us both for months.'

'Bloodhounds?' she queried.

'Members of Midas's staff who register as guests and observe how the hotel is being run, and then compile a financial and operational analysis,' he explained. 'The final decision is up to Scott Jeffreys, of course, but before he makes it he probably knows more about his prospective purchase than the owner!' He tapped a folder lying in front of him. 'He sent me this copy to read. It's quite something, Kate, and gave me an insight into the reason for his phenomenal success.' He studied the petite, grave-faced girl sitting on the other side of his desk. 'I know you came here because you didn't want to be part of a large organisation, but all the same, I hope you will stay on and work for Midas.'

Kate lowered her lids and long, dark copper lashes shaded her green eyes. 'I doubt it. Mr Jeffreys sounds like a typical brash American tycoon—all facts and figures and no heart.'

'He sees the hotel business differently from the way we do,' the elderly man agreed. 'But I'm afraid he's right. The day of the big independents is finished, and it's only the chain hotels who can show a reasonable profit. Streamlining and uniformity is the name of the game, and service and individuality are dirty words.'

He could not hide the bitterness from his voice, and it gave Kate the clue as to the true reason for the sale of the hotel. Blakes' reputation had always ranked with interna-tional hostelries like the George V in Paris, the Danieli in Venice and the Hôtel de Paris in Monte Carlo. It must be hard to accept that for all the prestige and glamour it still enjoyed, it had slipped behind them all. Not that the slippage was disastrous or could not be rectified, but it would need new financing and a new approach, and at seventy, these were beyond the capabilities of Roger Blake. His day was done, and he realised it.

'When will Midas be taking over?' she asked aloud.

'At the end of the month, and I'd like you to take until then to consider your position carefully. It appears you're one of the few of our staff who impressed Mr Jeffreys' bloodhounds, and he himself mentioned that he'd like you to stay on—although it might not be in quite the same capacity as now,' the hotelier added. 'Apparently they liked the way you handled the problem of an elderly woman diner who was placed next to the kitchen, when the restaurant was only half full—she happened to be a member of their team.'

Kate recalled the incident vividly, remembering how annoyed she had been at the time. Like so many hotels and restaurants, Blakes did not particularly care to serve women unaccompanied by men, tending to treat them like second-class citizens, and placing them at bad tables with poor service. On this occasion the elderly client had not only been alone but shabbily dressed, and the head waiter, sensing a set menu order and a small tip, had placed her next to the kitchen door, in spite of a half-empty dining room. Her meal was constantly disturbed by the to-ing and fro-ing of waiters, and Kate, seated nearby—she was allowed to eat her meals there at off-peak hours, as were all executives—had noticed the woman's discomfort. Not caring that she would arouse the head waiter's displeasure by going above him, she had sought out the restaurant's manager, and he had immediately moved the guest to a table by the window, and offered her a liqueur on the house by way of an apology.

'You're a bright girl, Kate, as well as a decorative one.' Roger Blake was speaking again. 'You could go far in an organisation like Midas. They have no prejudice against the advancement of women, and have several in quite senior positions.'

'I'll think about it, Mr Blake,' she said carefully. 'In the meantime, is there anything you want me to take care of?' She placed her notepad on her lap and sat, pencil poised, ready for dictation.

When she emerged from the study some half an hour later, she found Mike Wentworth, the assistant general manager, waiting in her office. A tall, lean man of thirty, with attractive even features, he had worked at Claridges and the Churchill before coming to Blakes three years ago.

'You're a dark horse,' he greeted her. 'Fancy not letting on about Midas!'

'It's as much a surprise to me as to you. It all happened while I was away.'

'In that case you're forgiven,' he smiled. 'Any word about how it's going to affect us all?'

'None, but Mr Blake's asked me to arrange an executive meeting in the boardroom for three o'clock, so I suppose he'll tell us then. I'm going to have the notice mimeographed and sent round right away.'

'How about lunching with me beforehand? I can't wait to find out if I have to compete for your affections with any handsome Italians!'

'There wasn't one man at the hotel who wasn't fat, fifty, bald and married!'

'In that case I win on all counts!'

Kate laughed. 'What time shall we meet?'

For the next hour she dealt with several queries that Janet had left for her to handle, and a press conference in the suite of a Hollywood actress who was in London to marry her fifth husband, twenty years her junior, kept Kate busy for the remainder of the morning. By two, with a headache caused by cigarette smoke and alcohol fumes, she would have preferred to spend her lunch hour quietly in her office. But a wash and fresh lipstick revived her flagging spirits, and when she entered the restaurant to join Mike, several pairs of male eyes followed her progress with interest as she crossed the room to their corner table.

Physically petite, she was exactly five feet two and perfectly proportioned, with beautifully shaped legs and the high insteps of a ballet dancer. High cheekbones, wide apart green eyes, a small nose covered with a sprinkling of freckles at the bridge, and a generously wide mouth with full lower lip, were features that needed little make-up to enhance them. But it was her copper-coloured hair that was her most noticeable asset. Worn page-boy style, so that it fell across her brow in a shiny fringe and then down her temples to rest sleekly on slender shoulders, it was a bright halo around her head and made her positively glow with life.

Her voice was soft, with a slight husky quality that was deceptive, for despite her gentle way of speaking she had a quick temper. Though she curbed it well, once in a while it served a purpose to get things done quickly, particularly around the hotel.

An only child of doting parents, her first job had been working for them in the small Georgian manor house in the Cotswolds, which they ran as a hotel. It would have been all too easy to listen to their pleas to make her stay a permanent one, but she knew that unless she broke away from their domination, they would completely smother her, and she had flown their luxurious coop and come to roost in a flat in Hampstead, which she shared with an old school friend.

Accepting the fact that she lived in London, and proud

that she held down such a responsible job, her parents still tended to spoil her when she returned home for the occasional weekend, and though it was fun to be pampered, with breakfast in bed and no washing up, it was equally pleasurable to return to Fitzjohn's Avenue, and the bustle of a top floor conversion in an Edwardian semi.

Now, seated across from Mike, Kate thought of her parents, and their fears when she had first told them she was moving away from home.

'Beware of the men,' her mother had warned. 'They'll all be after one thing, and it won't include a wedding ring!'

But how wrong she had been. There had been no lack of offers of the right kind, and it had been her own lack of interest in marriage that had been the cause of any trouble. As it was now with Mike, who proposed at least once a month and refused to take no for an answer.

'You look terribly serious.' He interrupted her thoughts as he caught her hand across the table. 'I hope you weren't thinking of me?'

'No,' she lied. 'I was thinking of all the changes that are going to take place once Midas takes over.'

He smiled ruefully. 'Then you're entitled to look serious. I don't think we're going to like most of them. From what I know of Midas they'll turn this place into an exact replica of every other one of their hotels from here to Timbuctoo!'

Kate disengaged her hand gently and picked up the menu. 'If their success is anything to go by, that's what the public wants. Do you know anything about the boss-man?'

'Only what I've read. He was something of a whizz-kid when he started twelve years ago.'

'A riches to riches, or rags to riches whizz-kid?' Kate asked:

'It seems he made it all on his own. The story goes that he worked as a junior assistant manager in a large hotel in Miami that was on the verge of bankruptcy. He managed to persuade their bankers that he could reverse its fortunes if he was given a free hand, and within eighteen months he had. From there, as they say, he never looked back.'

Kate looked suitably impressed. 'Mr Blake has asked me to stay on, but I don't know if I will.'

The head waiter appeared to take their order, and as soon as he had left, Mike picked up the conversation where they had left off.

'Do you think Midas will want to make many staff changes?'

'I don't know what the usual form is, but in any case, I'm sure your job's safe. You're the best assistant manager we've had in years,' Kate assured him.

'I wish I could share your confidence. The hotel's losing money, and someone has to take the blame.'

'It's hardly your fault,' Kate protested, knowing of Mike's constant frustration regarding inefficiencies within the hotel, which he lacked the authority to change. In a normally run establishment, with clear-cut lines of command, there would be no such problems. But at Blakes, the final responsibility lay with Roger Blake, and because of his outdated approach, his opinions often differed from Mike's. There had been several stormy scenes between them, and it had often fallen on Kate to act as mediator.

'I only hope Mr Jeffreys realises how tied my hands were,' Mike said.

'If I'm still here when he takes over, I'll put in a good word for you,' Kate teased.

'With your salary and perks you'd find it difficult to find another job as well paid as this one.'

'Money isn't everything,' Kate declared airily, though

she knew what Mike said was true. Roger Blake was an extremely generous employer, which was one of the reasons why, unlike many of his competitors, he had no difficulty in finding and keeping staff.

'That's because you can afford to be independent,' Mike pointed out, then added: 'I know you haven't taken a penny from your parents since you left home, but if it came to the crunch . . .'

'It wouldn't make any difference if they were poor,' Kate answered defensively. 'If I don't like Scott Jeffreys, I shan't stay here.'

'This place won't be the same without you,' he murmured, as their lobster salads arrived.

'In three weeks' time when Midas take over, this place won't be the same with me!' she declared. 'Scott Jeffreys will see to that!'

By the time they arrived in the boardroom, nearly all the seats were occupied, and promptly at three Roger Blake appeared. Somehow in a few hours he seemed to have aged ten years. Deep lines were carved down the side of his nose, and there were shadows beneath his eyes. Kate's heart went out to him, knowing how he must have been dreading this moment when he had to face his many elderly and loyal employees, most of whom he looked upon as friends. He himself had hired them when they were all young, and had it not been for his kind heart they would have been retired years ago. But the new owner wouldn't feel the same loyalty, and they would be forced into retirement; a slow death to those who only lived for the hours they spent at Blakes.

Roger Blake's voice, as he began to explain the reasons for the takeover, cut across her thoughts, and though conversant with the facts already, she gave him her undivided attention.

'As for your future,' he ended, 'I can only quote Mr Jeffreys. There will be no immediate staff changes.'

'I've heard that song before,' the head barman, standing behind Kate, muttered. 'They always announce that there won't be any staff changes, and as soon as they move in, they get on with the firings.'

'If I hear of something in the meanwhile, I'll grab it,' the room service manager agreed.

As others joined in, the babble of voices grew louder, and Roger Blake held up his hands.

'I know it's not very satisfactory, but I'm afraid there was no way Mr Jeffreys was prepared to give guarantees. He will be running the hotel his way, and many of you may find that it's not to your liking. It will be up to you to decide what to do. But my advice is—give him a chance. From my own dealings with him, I can assure you he's a fair and honourable man.'

'That's what they said about Brutus,' a derisive shout came from the back, 'and look what he did!'

There was little the elderly man could add, in spite of a barrage of questions, and the meeting broke up soon afterwards.

'That was a complete waste of time,' Mike grumbled as they stood waiting for the lift to take them back to their respective offices. 'No one's any the wiser about where they stand than before.'

It was easy to understand his anxiety. If he were fired by Midas he would not find it easy to secure a position of equal status. And unlike herself, he had no family money or business to fall back on. An orphan, he had learned his trade the hard way, beginning in the kitchens, and graduating from dogsbody to top dog. To look at him now, no one would guess at his humble origins: with his smooth, well-trimmed dun hair, neatly clipped moustache and upright bearing, he could easily have been taken for an ex-Guards officer. His voice too, was as cultivated as his appearance, and she guessed a good percentage of his salary went to a Savile Row tailor.

Yet so much of Mike was a facade that it was difficult to know what lay behind it. The first time he kissed her had afforded her one, for he had shown an almost savage passion that surprised her as much as it had scared her. Even now, though he was more careful, there was still little tenderness in his caress, and enough force in his lips to bruise her.

'How about dinner tonight?' he asked, as they entered the lift. 'I could do with cheering up.'

Although Kate had half promised to eat with her flatmate, he looked so depressed that she did not have the heart to refuse. Thrown together at work, they also spent a couple of evenings a week together. It was a habit he refused to let her break, although she had made it abundantly clear that she was not in love with him and did not think it fair to monopolise his time.

'I'll stop asking you out when you tell me you're in love with someone else,' he had replied. And because he knew this had not yet happened, he continued to see her.

He was an amusing companion, and one with whom she was never at a loss for words: though now she came to think of it, they rarely discussed anything other than Blakes.

'I thought we'd try Angelino's.' He mentioned a restaurant that had opened to great acclaim a couple of months ago. 'Unless after three weeks in Italy you're tired of pasta?' he added.

'I've been wanting to try it,' she said, 'and I never tire of Italian food. I adore it!'

'I wish your eyes glowed as brightly when you spoke

about me!' he replied. 'I'd be much better for you than a plate of lasagna!'

She laughed, and linked her arm with his in a companionable gesture as they walked down the corridor towards her office. It was a gesture Kate instantly regretted, for he immediately mistook it for something more intimate.

'I think absence *has* made your heart grow fonder,' he said huskily, and glancing to left and right to make sure there was no one else about, he pulled her into his arms. His kiss was deep and fierce, as always, and she struggled against it, conscious of the hardness of his cheekbones, the prickly feel of his moustache, and the sharp but not unpleasing smell of his after-shave lotion.

'Why don't you let yourself go, Kate?' he asked as he released her.

'In the corridor?' she teased, not wishing to be too hard on him.

'You're the same wherever I kiss you.'

'That's because you frighten me.'

Mike brightened, reading a quite different meaning into her remark. But before she could say anything else, a door at the far end opened and one of the cost clerks emerged.

'I'll pick you up at eight,' said Mike. 'We'll go to Les A' for a drink first.'

Not for the first time Kate marvelled that he could afford to spend so extravagantly. His salary was a good one, and he was a bachelor. But he ran an expensive sports car and shared a fashionable and expensive pad in World's End, Chelsea, with a stockbroker friend. She had once asked him—her nature was nothing if not blunt— and he had told her his friend provided him with tips on shares.

His friend must be something of a genius, she mused, as she settled behind her desk. Because of his advice, Mike lived well and had an upper-crust circle of intimates, weekending at their country homes and spending holidays abroad at fashionable resorts. Perhaps there was no need for him to look worried. If he did lose his job, with his knack for investments he could go into the stock market full time and make a fortune.

But Mike was soon banished from her thoughts by the pressure of work. The newspapers had been bombarding Mr Blake for a statement since early morning and he had asked her to arrange a press conference for later that day.

It gave her the opportunity to question the reporters about Scott Jeffreys, and she was pleasantly surprised to find that their opinion of him was unanimously high.

Not everyone liked his entrepreneurial style, and the fact that he was inclined to ride roughshod over anyone who disagreed with him. But unlike so many conglomerates, the dealings of his companies were always above board, and he did not try to exploit the staff of his hotels in some of the poorer countries. If he could not make a fair profit by paying them a fair wage, he preferred not to open there in the first place. It did not make him popular with some of the other multi-nationals, but he was important enough and influential enough to be able to stick to his principles, whatever the pressure to dissuade him.

It was a warming picture, though Kate could not entirely dismiss his comments in this morning's newspapers. There were bound to be changes at Blakes—he had made that quite clear. But they might not necessarily all be for the worse. Perhaps he would find it possible to make the hotel profitable without making it conform to the plasticity and uniformity of the others in the Midas group. In the light of what she had learned about him, it was worth waiting to see rather than prejudge the issue. If she *was* unhappy with the changes, or with Mr Jeffreys, she could always hand in her notice.

CHAPTER TWO

THE next few weeks flew by. Never would Kate have believed there was so much work involved in passing a hotel over from one owner to another. The lawyers might be involved with the legal niceties and twenty-page contracts, but there were hundreds of items to be accounted for that could not be set out on paper.

Though Roger Blake had sold the hotel as it stood, Scott Jeffreys was allowing him to take any personal items he wished, and had been generous enough not to put a limit on their price.

'Not that I want to take away anything valuable,' the older man said. 'Merely things that have sentimental memories for me. Like the chandelier in my office; the china and silver used in my personal suite, and all the ornaments, of course.'

Kate had laughed at this, for Roger Blake's predeliction for colourful knick-knacks had been a joke among his staff.

The day of his departure they had all gathered in the ballroom to bid him goodbye, and there had been no lack of tears after he had made his moving farewell speech. He too had been moved, particularly by the beautiful slim gold Cartier pen, embossed with the hotel's crest, which the senior staff had presented to him.

Afterwards, alone with Kate in his office, he had confided his regrets that he had sold out.

'Maybe if I'd hung on, put word around that I was willing to take in some younger partners—even given Mike Wentworth a chance to show more of his mettle . . .'

'It wouldn't have worked,' said Kate. 'Once you'd brought in a lot of other people it would no longer have been your hotel. It was having you at the helm that made this place so special, and if you had to bring in new faces, then it was just as well to pull out completely.'

'What a practical girl you are,' Roger Blake said admiringly. 'No one would think it from looking at you.'

'You still see me as a little doll in a toy-shop, don't you?' Kate grinned. 'If I were five feet eight and officious-looking—'

'You wouldn't be the Kate I know,' he chuckled, then sobered as he went on: 'Don't leave here without giving Midas a chance. I know they won't run the hotel the way I do, but at least if you're here, you might be able to persuade them to be a little less conformist than normal.

'I'm no Canute, Mr Blake. Once Midas are in control I'll be surprised if they don't turn this hotel into a copy of every other place they own.'

'They might make it their flagship.'

'They might,' Kate conceded. But in her heart of hearts she doubted it. An American group like Midas would want their flagship hotel to be in the States. Yet she did not have the heart to tell this to the grey-haired man in front of her who, even now, was slipping into his topcoat and preparing to leave this suite of rooms for the last time. Briskly he went down the corridor to the lift, then through the lobby to his car, looking neither to right nor left, and merely acknowledging the last goodbyes with the faintest of smiles.

Only when he reached the car and sank into the back seat did the sigh that escaped him tell Kate what an effort he had found it to maintain his equilibrium.

'I won't come back here again,' he said quietly. 'Never.'

'Never's a long time, Mr Blake.'

'I suppose so.' He caught her hand. 'But I won't be losing touch with you, my dear. And if ever you need any advice, or want any help, don't hesitate to give me a call.'

Promising she would, Kate watched the Rolls bear him out of sight. His departure was the end of an era, not only for Blakes, but for herself too.

On the Thursday morning a phone call from the Midas head office in Miami informed her that Mr Jeffreys' personal workmen would be arriving to redecorate the suite that Roger Blake had occupied.

'It's going to be some time before all the alterations to the hotel are completed,' a businesslike man with a nasal twang had informed her, 'and we always like to get Mr Jeffreys' private quarters done first, so that he can move in and be on the spot to supervise things.'

'Did you say his own workmen?' Kate questioned, sensing union troubles ahead of her.

'Yes. But don't worry, there'll be a standby British crew being paid, even though they won't be doing the work.'

'Isn't that rather a waste of—'

'No,' the man interrupted, as if he had been asked this question many times before. 'Mr Jeffreys is very particular about everything, and all his suites have to be identical, so that whenever he moves from one to another, he knows that everything is going to be in the same place.'

'Like the Holiday Inn group?'

'Right,' the man laughed. 'Only with Mr Jeffreys it's even more so.'

Before Kate could ask what he meant, he had terminated the call, leaving her to warn the staff of the impending arrival of the personal workforce.

For most of the weekend Kate found herself thinking about the hotel, and wondering how she would feel when she walked into Roger Blake's suite and found it furnished in Mr Jeffreys' style. Heaven knew what that would be —imitation antique, or else garish modern. She caught herself up. There was no need to fan her dislike of him. If she intended to give it a try to go on working for him she had to watch her prejudice—and certainly stop it from showing. In fact, Mike said as much to her when he took her out for dinner on Saturday.

'Be like me,' he warned. 'Keep your thoughts to yourself and do your best to please your bosses. Don't forget a new broom sweeps clean, and if we can keep out of the way of the bristles for the first six months, we might end up home and dry.'

'I don't think you've anything to worry about, Mike. You're good at your job—as I've already told you.'

'I'd rather you told me you'd marry me.' He reached across the table and caught hold of her hand. 'You must know how I feel about you, Kate. I've made it as obvious as you'd let me.'

'Oh, Mike!' She looked at him helplessly, not wanting to hurt him, yet not wanting to make a commitment she could not follow through. 'I don't know what to say.'

'You could say yes.'

'I don't think I'm in love with you.'

'Why don't you say, I think I'm not in love with you? At least be negative in a positive way!'

Kate laughed, her tension evaporating. As long as Mike played the game lightly, she would not feel guilty at continuing to see him. But should he persist in wanting a firm answer from her, then it would regretfully have to be no. At least that was how she felt at the moment. Maybe I'm not the type who'll ever be completely bowled over by a man, she thought, and wondered what it was she was actually looking for. A dominant personality to sweep her off her feet? Yet that sort of man would want to rule her life too, and she was far too independent for that. Then how about someone who was willing to settle for a fifty-fifty relationship? That was the ideal, of course. But how few men were ideal—and women too, for that matter! Each person wanted what was best for themselves, and it was rare for two people to meet and find their ideas coincided. They did with her parents, of course, and maybe that was another reason for her hesitation over Mike. Witnessing the loving relationship that existed between them, even after twenty-five years of marriage, had no doubt made her unwilling to settle for anything less than perfection, and since perfection was well nigh impossible to find, it was quite on the cards that she would end up with a compromise. But not yet. There was always time for that.

'Fancy going on somewhere to dance?' Mike asked.

Knowing that if they did he would end up drinking more than was good for him, which would also make him become more amorous than was good for her, she declined, pretending she was leaving London early the following morning to spend the day with her parents.

Though none too pleased at having to leave her outside her door before midnight—Kate rarely let Mike into the apartment unless Lucy was there too—he was careful not to show it, and with a quick but passionate embrace, left her at the front door. That was another surprising thing about Mike. He occasionally didn't act true to form. Like tonight, for instance, when she had expected him to plead to be allowed in for a coffee—which would have ended up with his trying to make love to her. Yet instead he had accepted her rebuff without question, which had made her feel guilty for ending their evening so early. Perhaps it was this very facet of Mike's nature—his ability to do the unexpected—that made her occasionally wary of him, and gave her the feeling that he might be putting on an act with her. Yet didn't men and women do this with each other the whole time? She was pondering over this question when she fell asleep and did not awaken until the ringing of the telephone penetrated her unconscious. Struggling awake, and blinking against the autumn sunlight shining through her undrawn curtains, she reached for the telephone.

It was Mr Blake, apologising for disturbing her at the weekend, but asking her if she would go into his office first thing on Monday to retrieve the gold presentation pen that had been given to him by the staff.

'It wasn't until late last night when I went to show it to someone that I realised I'd left it in my desk drawer. I can't think how it happened. I didn't want to ring the manager, and admit to it, so I was wondering—'

'I'll go to the hotel today and collect it,' Kate cut in quickly, knowing how embarrassed her erstwhile employer would be should the senior staff discover he had forgotten to take their gift home with him.

Gratefully Roger Blake hung up. Kate had a leisurely breakfast, enjoyed herself reading the gossip columns, then showered and slipped into a casual autumn suit before driving down the quiet streets and through the park to the hotel.

Because it was Sunday she did not bother leaving her car in the private car park, but left it by the kerb and went briskly through the lobby to the elevator, eschewing the staff entrance. After all, it was Sunday and her day off, so to hell with it.

There were plenty of guests milling about, and people were already coming in to sample the Sunday lunch for

which the hotel was justifiably famous. That would probably go once Midas were in full control, Kate thought,
stepping out on to the top floor and making her way to the
corner penthouse suite. Even as she approached it she
heard the sound of hammering, and a cheery voice raised
in song. Frowning, she ran the last few steps and pushed
open the door. An astonishing sight met her eyes. Gone
was the beautiful panelling that had covered all the walls
of the lobby and large sitting room, whose windows looked
out over the river. The timber lay in torn strips on the
floor, and the walls, rough and raw-looking, were already
being sanded smooth. Indeed one section had already
been done, and was covered by thick hessian, in a subtle
shade of palest silver-grey that matched—Kate saw with
astonishment—the ceiling and woodwork. Heavens
above, this little task force must have been hard at it night
and day since Friday evening! Anxiously she stepped
forward, stopping with relief as she saw that the ornate
desk which Mr Blake had used had been shifted to the far
corner and was partially covered by a dust-sheet. Only
partially, though, for one corner had been shoved aside
and the drawer opened by the tall wide-shouldered man
who was studying it curiously. Kate continued to walk
forward and as she neared him saw the gold pen for which
she had come sticking blatantly out of his breast pocket.

'I think you've got something that belongs to me,' she
said sweetly.

The man lifted his head and straightened, then looked
down at her. He had a long way to look, for he was well
over six foot with a physique to match. He must have been
a basketball player, she thought, or a lumberjack, with
those shoulders. There was certainly a rugged outdoor air
about him that was echoed in the craggy features—wide
mouth, dominant nose and alert brown eyes, marked by

faint lines as if he were used to screwing them up against the sun. A roughneck, she thought. Yet not quite, for his smile held an easy confidence that came from giving commands: obviously the foreman.

'I'd like it back,' she continued, holding out her hand.

'Like what back?' His voice fitted him perfectly, being deep and drawling, yet incisive.

'The pen you've got in your breast pocket.' She pointed at it. 'It isn't yours.'

'How do I know it's *yours*?'

She coloured. 'It actually belongs to Mr Blake, and I've come to collect it for him.'

'You mean the old boy left it behind? No wonder he couldn't make a go of the hotel!'

'That's got nothing to do with it,' she snapped. 'He happened to be in a very emotional state of mind when it was given to him.'

'Drunk, you mean?'

'Certainly not! Do you always see the nasty side to everything?'

''Fraid I do. I'm a realist.'

'Then be a realist and give me the pen,' she said crossly.

'I wasn't planning on stealing it, lady.'

'I'm glad to hear it.'

Still he did not take the pen out of his breast pocket but went on staring at her. Refusing to be embarrassed by the intentness of his stare, she did the same to him, though she felt somewhat at a disadvantage because she had to tilt her head quite a way to get him in her sights. Close up he was a formidable hunk of man, for all that his boiler suit was the most ill-fitting she had seen.

'Are you part of the contingent that's come over to alter the suite for Mr Jeffreys?' she asked.

'What?' He looked at her in surprise.

'Are you in charge of these workmen?' she repeated.

'You could say that.'

'I'd rather you said it. I assume you have a pass to give you authority to come into the hotel?'

'I'm no thief, lady, for all I've got the pen in my pocket.' Laconically he took it out and passed it over to her.

'I didn't think you were,' she said coolly, curling the pen between her fingers. There was nothing to keep her here any longer, yet for some reason she was reluctant to go. 'What are you doing to this room?' she asked.

'Everything. It's a mess as it is.'

'It wasn't, until you started ripping out the panelling.'

'That old timber?'

'That old timber, as you call it, happened to be beautiful walnut.'

'Each to his taste, lady, and it doesn't happen to be mine.'

Kate eyed every foot of him coolly, from the top of his thick dark brown hair that rose in an aggressive sweep above his forehead to the dust-coated shoes covering his feet.

Aware of her gaze, he straightened his shoulders, and the paint-spattered boiler-suit stretched ominously tight.

'Don't tell me Mr Jeffreys relies on your taste?' she said sweetly.

'As a matter of fact he does. He wouldn't move a step without me.'

'Really?'

'Sure thing.'

'And what—as Mr Jeffreys' alter ego—are you planning to do to this suite?'

'Well, as you can see, we've ripped out all the timber and are bringing the whole thing back into the twentieth century. I—Mr Jeffreys, that is—feels there's no point in living in today's world and looking back into yesterday's.'

'You mean nothing of yesterday's is any good?'

'I didn't say that, lady,' he drawled, 'Some antique pieces are great. But he just feels happier around modern stuff. A question of use, I guess.'

'Of course. Coming up the hard way, I don't suppose he was used to good things as a child.'

'Were you?' he asked insolently.

Aware that she had spoken as a snob and ashamed of it, Kate coloured. 'Actually I was. I don't mean to sound snobbish, Mr er—I'm afraid I don't know your name.'

'I don't know yours either, or who you are. Maybe you're a thief come in to see what you could lay your hands on.'

'Really!' she gasped angrily.

'You mean I guessed right?'

'Of course you didn't guess right,' she said indignantly. 'I'm Kate Ashton and I'm personal assistant to Mr Jeffreys.'

One thick eyebrow was raised in query.

'You know him, then?'

She hesitated, but then decided on the truth. 'Not yet, but—'

'Then you can't be his personal assistant. He'd never hire someone he hadn't met for that sort of position. Now be truthful, lady. What do you do here? Maid service, or some other kind of service?'

'I was Roger Blake's personal assistant,' she said icily, 'and until I'm fired, I remain personal assistant to the owner of this hotel—who happens to be Mr Scott Jeffreys. Where's *your* identification?'

Before he could answer she swung round and pointed her hand towards a young workman walking swiftly through the room carrying a large pot of paint and a spray gun. 'Do you know this man?' she asked, indicating the wide-shouldered figure behind her.

'Sure I do.' The young man looked startled. 'He's my boss.'

Discomfited, Kate swung back to look at the foreman.

'Your suspicions at rest?' he asked softly, looking all the way down his nose at her. 'For a little bit of a thing, you're very aggressive.'

'Don't be personal!'

'Okay, Miss Giant. What else can I do for you?'

There was nothing, in fact, and she knew she should go. But curiosity made her linger. 'How are you decorating the other rooms?' she asked.

'Come and take a look,' he invited. Kate followed him across the sitting room into the bedroom. Expecting to see the same dissarray, she was astonished to find it was completely finished, and could have been a photograph taken from the latest design magazine. From the apricot-washed walls to the thick tan carpet, tan and white curtains, and large circular bed, with suede-covered head-board and bedside tables, it was a picture of everything modern man—or woman for that matter—could have desired. There were even pictures on the walls—A Debufy, a charming Hockney flower painting, its stark simplicity making it masculine rather than feminine, and an aggressive abstract which she did not recognise. Mr Jeffreys had expensive taste, she thought, moving forward for a better look at the Hockney. Not until she reached it did she see that it was an excellent copy; set on to canvas with each stroke visible, the colours brilliantly exact. Yet it was still a copy.

'Can't he afford the originals?' she asked, looking at the foreman.

'The originals hang in his home in Longboat Key.'

'Longboat where?'

'In Florida, where he lives, lady. This suite duplicates the bedroom and private sitting room in his house. He has the same suite in each of his hotels.'

'You're joking!' she protested.

'What's funny about it? It strikes me it's the most efficient way of carrying on. Like this, no matter which of his hotels he's staying at, he feels at home.'

'Except that his home must also feel like his hotels.'

'That's a point,' the foreman said thoughtfully. 'I think he's just beginning to realise it. However, it does have advantages, rushing round from Miami to Los Angeles to Tokyo, to Honolulu, Sydney, Rome, etcetera, etcetera. It can make you very disoriented, and entering a suite of rooms with which you're familiar has very special psychological benefits. This way he knows where everything is, even his suits.'

'You mean he has his wardrobe duplicated too?'

'Ten times over,' came the reply. 'He only stays at his top ten hotels for any length of time. The vanguard of his fleet, you might say.'

'So there are ten copies of his paintings?'

'Everything's identical, down to the toothbrush.'

Remembering the little she knew of Scott Jeffreys, Kate found the whole idea amusing. 'What about his girlfriends?' she smiled. 'Are they all identical too?'

'When it comes to women, Mr Jeffreys likes variety.'

'As long as they're all dumb and blonde, I suppose! They're the kind middle-aged tycoons generally prefer, aren't they?'

'I thought you said you didn't know Mr Jeffreys?'

'I don't.'

'Then how come you know he's middle-aged, and what his taste in women is?'

'He began as a whizz-kid, and that was twelve years ago, so he must be in his forties,' Kate pointed out.

'And you'd call that middle-aged?' The brown eyes surveyed her. They were so dark a brown that his pupils were not discernible, and gave his stare an intentness she had not seen in any other man. 'I suppose to a kid like you any man over thirty would be middle-aged.'

'I'm not a kid,' she snapped, her good humour vanishing. 'I'm twenty-three.'

'You don't look a day over eighteen. That must be because you're half-pint sized.'

She drew herself up to every inch of her five feet two. 'There's no need to be personal, Mr—er—I still don't know your name.'

'Call me darling. All my girl-friends do.'

Ignoring the comment, she swept out of the room. The spray-gun was already busy at work in the sitting room, and she was sure that by this evening, this room too would be a perfect replica of all the others Mr Jeffreys lived in. The lack of imagination it showed was horrendous, even though she appreciated the reasons behind it.

'At least he could vary the pictures,' she said, looking at the foreman, who was standing close beside her. Too close, she thought, stepping back quickly, and nearly putting her foot into a bucket of paint.

'Watch out!' he warned, grabbing her fast in an iron-handed grip that was bone-shattering. 'I'm used to my women falling at my feet, but not into a paint-pot!'

'You're insufferably conceited,' she said, pulling free of him.

'Because I know women want me?'

'What sort of women?' she retorted. 'Imbeciles?'

He grinned, showing perfect white teeth. It made him

look much younger, in his middle thirties perhaps, but it did not detract from his aggressive air, and she knew he was not a man to cross. I wouldn't like to work for him, she thought. He wouldn't brook argument, nor would he be easy to persuade. 'How long have you been with Mr Jeffreys?' she asked, changing the subject.

'For as long as I can remember.'

'You mean you've had no other job?'

The brown eyes looked at her searchingly. 'Are you always so curious about the hired help, lady?'

Knowing he had a good point, and furious that she had left herself open to such a comment, she flushed.

'Very pretty,' he drawled. 'I've never gone in for little women, but I might change my mind with you.'

'Opportunity would be a fine thing, Mr Darling. But you're not likely to get it with me.'

'I guess not,' he said abruptly. 'I can't see you having much in common with a hired hand.'

'That wouldn't be the reason at all. I'm not a snob,' she emphasised again.

'Aren't you? Tell me, Miss Ashton, how many working class men have you dated?'

'All the men I date work.'

'That wasn't the question I asked.'

'Well, it's the only answer you're going to get. All these questions about class are nonsensical.'

'They still apply, though. Rich little society girls want rich little society boys, though they'll make the exception if the roughneck happens to be even more loaded than they are.'

'That's a very cynical comment,' she observed.

'It's realistic, and as I've told you before, I'm a realist. Which reminds me, I can't stand here wasting any more time with you, gorgeous though you are.'

Colouring again, Kate went swiftly to the door. 'I'm so sorry to take up your time,' she said dulcetly, 'but I had to make sure you weren't a thief.'

'I only steal pretty girls' hearts.'

Sniffing, she walked out, but once in the corridor, couldn't help grinning. If all the American staff Mr Jeffreys brought over were epitomised by the one she had just left, the present employees at Blakes hotel were going to find themselves in for quite an exciting time! Still, she was the first to admit that there had to be changes made here if the hotel were to continue to function as a first-class entity, and it would be as well to hold herself in readiness for the upheaval that was bound to come.

She could understand now why Roger Blake had said he would never set foot inside the hotel again, for if the alterations to his penthouse suite were anything to go by, Blakes would be unrecognisable by the time Scott Jeffreys had finished with it. Was *he* the sort of man to command his staff's affection? she wondered, and reached into her handbag to make sure her erstwhile employer's gold presentation pen was safe. But it wasn't there. Momentarily she panicked, but then remembered she had put it down on one of the suede-covered bedside tables when the foreman had been showing her around. Damn. It would mean going back, and he was conceited enough to think she had forgotten it on purpose, so that she had an excuse to return.

Retracing her footsteps, she opened the door to the suite, but though several of the workmen turned to look at her, there was no sign of their foreman. Perhaps he'd used the back exit to nip out for a cup of coffee—or something stronger. Breathing a sigh of relief, she entered the bedroom.

'Couldn't resist coming back to see me, eh, beautiful?'

The voice of the man she had hoped to avoid drawled lazily from the bed.

'I left Mr Blake's pen behind.' Kate ignored his comment, and picked it up to show him. He was lying with his head propped against the apricot suede bedhead, and though he had removed his dust-covered shoes, his overalls were not exactly in pristine condition either. 'Do you think Mr Jeffreys would approve of you using his bed?' she asked. 'Your clothes aren't exactly spick and span.'

'Frankly I'm too tired to care. The time change is beginning to catch up with me.'

'Your workmen must be just as tired, but they're managing to soldier on,' Kate pointed out drily.

'They arrived on Thursday, so they've had plenty of time to adjust, whereas I flew in late yesterday,' he explained, unperturbed by her criticism.

'Didn't you sleep at all last night?'

'Only for a couple of hours. I bunked down here, and then the night crew disturbed me when they started hammering.'

'I wouldn't have thought it much better now,' she said. 'Surely it would be more sensible to take a nap somewhere quieter.'

'Where do you suggest?' he smiled. 'Your place, perhaps?'

Kate felt her cheeks redden. 'Only if you fancy sleeping on the floor,' she said flippantly. 'Where are you supposed to be staying?'

'My men are in the staff quarters here, but unfortunately they haven't room for me at the moment.'

'Surely you could double up with one of them?'

He shrugged, and swung long legs on to the floor. 'I like my privacy, and besides, I might decide I want female company once I get over the time change.'

Kate's colour deepened. 'In that case, you certainly can't stay here.'

'Then what do you suggest I do?'

'I'm sure I can manage to swing a room for you in the hotel itself. But just for tonight,' she added hastily. 'Tomorrow, you'll have to find yourself other accommodation.'

'I'm sure when Mr Jeffreys arrives he'll sort something out for me.'

'He'll be very busy, so I don't suppose he'll want to be bothered with your problems,' she said sarcastically. 'I suggest you find something yourself. There are plenty of bed and breakfast places nearby and they're quite reasonable.'

'Yes, ma'am,' he answered meekly, but his brown eyes were full of amusement.

'If you come with me now, I'll have a word with the booking clerk,' she ordered briskly.

After a few minutes' consultation with his crew, he accompanied her down to the vestibule, where Tom Riley, the booking clerk, happily obliged her with a key to an empty room on the first floor.

'You've been very kind, Miss Ashton,' the broad-shouldered man said. 'Perhaps I could buy you a drink,' he glanced at his watch, 'or even lunch, to show my appreciation.'

'I'm afraid I haven't time for either. I was due at some friends' ten minutes ago.'

'Some other time, then? Tuesday, perhaps?'

'I—' She was about to make an excuse, but then remembered his remark about her not wishing to go out with a hired hand. If she refused him, it would confirm his suspicion that she was a snob, though why she should care what he thought of her, she did not stop to think.

'I'd like that. Where shall we meet?'

'How about trying our competition up the road? I'll book a table for lunch, and meet you in the Savoy bar at one.'

Kate hesitated. 'I—I er—don't know how well you know London, but the Savoy is frightfully expensive,' she said finally, deciding bluntness now might save embarrassment later. 'If I allow you to pay for the drinks, will you let me split the bill for lunch? I'd be happier going Dutch.'

Hands in his pockets, he teetered on his heels and looked at her. 'But I wouldn't. I'm the old-fashioned type. Anyway, I'm well aware of the prices at the Savoy, and if I couldn't afford them I wouldn't have suggested taking you there.'

His tone left no room for argument. 'Till Tuesday, then, Mr—?' She looked at him quizzically.

'Darling will continue to do nicely.' He grinned mischievously. 'Most English girls are about as forthcoming as frozen fillets, so it's nice to have broken the ice with one so quickly!'

'Perhaps you've tried to heat them up too hurriedly. They respond better to careful handling.'

'Does that apply to you too?' he asked softly.

'You'll find that out when you get to know me better—darling!' Kate was annoyed to find her voice breathless, as though she'd been running.

His wide mouth parted in a grin. 'I like the way you answer back, pint pot.'

'I prefer Kate, if you don't mind,' she smiled back. 'Well, if I don't see you before—'

'I shall make a point of seeing that you do,' he said gravely, and accompanied her to the entrance.

Aware he was watching her through the glass doors, she

made her way back to her car. What an unusual man he was! Certainly like no foreman she had ever met before. Far more sophisticated and in command of himself, with not the slightest trace of subservience. Attractive too, and as for his build—she had felt like a midget beside him. But tall men often liked petite girls. He was probably the type who liked all girls, she thought practically, and he would certainly have no shortage of followers.

'Snap out of it, Kate,' she ordered herself. 'You've spent the best part of the journey thinking about a man whose name you don't even know, and who probably hasn't given you a second thought.' In fact, he was probably fast asleep by now. He had certainly looked tired. She slowed, and then shook her head in puzzlement. It was strange that there was no room in the staff quarters for him. Surely they'd been aware of his arrival? Strange too, the way he had assumed Scott Jeffreys would take care of his accommodation. But then he had obviously known the man a long time, so perhaps their relationship was rather more personal than employer and employee. In that case, it was fortunate that her comments about the hotel's new owner had not been more disparaging. No doubt loyalty would have demanded that 'Darling' repeat them.

She must remember to cancel her Tuesday date with Mike. He would not be pleased, particularly when he learned why. Still, he had no need to be jealous of the stranger. He would be returning to the States as soon as his work on the hotel was finished, so whatever turn their relationship took it would only be a brief encounter.

CHAPTER THREE

THE following morning the hotel was buzzing with the news of Scott Jeffreys' arrival. It appeared he had turned up unexpectedly, to supervise the refurnishing of his suite, but until Wednesday, the official date of the takeover, he, and other members of his entourage, were staying at the Connaught.

'Did you get to meet him?' Kate asked Mike, knowing he had been on duty Sunday evening.

'We had quite a chat, as it happens, and I have to admit I was most impressed. He's high-powered all right but can turn on the charm as well.'

'The same could be said of you,' Kate smiled. 'Did he give any hints as to whether he's going to make any changes at managerial level?'

'He made a point of bringing it up, and he more or less reiterated what Mr Blake said. He intends to leave things as they are for a while—to give everyone a chance to show their mettle under Midas.'

'In that case, I'm sure you have nothing to worry about.'

Mike smiled his agreement. 'How about helping me celebrate? A friend has given me two tickets to the opening of "More the Merrier".' He named a musical that had been a smash hit on Broadway for the past two years, and had now transferred to London, complete with its original cast. 'He's down with 'flu, and can't use them himself.'

'I'd love to go,' said Kate. 'I've never been to a premiere before. What time must I be ready?'

'I'll collect you at seven-thirty—we'll eat afterwards.'

Deciding this was not the time to tell Mike about her luncheon date with the foreman decorating Scott Jeffreys' suite, she said instead:

'How shall I dress? Long?'

Mike nodded. 'I'm wearing a dinner suit, so I guess it would be appropriate.'

At seven-fifteen Kate was already dressed and waiting. No one looking at her would have believed she had spent a long and busy day at the office, where, to her disappointment, there had been no sign of the foreman. In her ivory crêpe-de-chine dress of pure silk, with full skirt, Victorian lace-trimmed bodice, and waist tightly sashed in blue satin, she looked like Alice in Wonderland. Mike said it too, as he greeted her with a kiss.

'You must be the most innocent-looking twenty-three-year-old in London,' he smiled, as he helped settle her skirts comfortably about her in the cramped front seat of his Porsche.

'That's because I am innocent,' she laughed, and although that was true, she doubted Mike would take her comment seriously.

Because of traffic congestion, they had to park some way from the theatre, and go on foot along Shaftesbury Avenue.

'I've booked a table at the White Elephant,' Mike told her, as they pushed their way through the throng of people milling outside the brilliantly lit foyer, banked with flowers for the special occasion.

'Sounds lovely. We'll probably see half tonight's audience there too.' Kate blinked as several flashlights went off in her eyes. Around her people were cheering and she watched a crowd of fans throng forward to greet a celebrity emerging from the back of a Rolls-Royce.

'Want to stand and gawk,' Mike enquired, 'or go inside and take our seats?'

'Let's gawk,' she suggested. 'In spite of all the celebrities I've met at Blakes, I still enjoy star-gazing!'

A young couple came towards them with a cry of recognition. They were Carol and Trevor Harper, married friends of Mike's, whom Kate had met several times and liked. Trevor, who was in computers, had worked in the States for a year, and had only recently returned to England.

'Have the Royals arrived yet?' Carol asked.

'We've only just got here ourselves,' Kate replied. 'But I don't think so.'

'What are you doing after the show?' Mike asked them. 'If you're on your own, how about joining us for dinner? I'm sure they'll be able to squeeze you round our table at the White Elephant.'

Trevor nodded. 'Sounds great. We'd—'

Another cheer from the crowd drowned the rest of what he was saying, and Kate, knowing she was not tall enough to see over the heads of the people in front of her, waited patiently for the celebrities to come within range of where she was standing.

'Boy, in the flesh, she's really something!' Trevor said admiringly.

'Who is?' Kate asked, wishing she were six inches taller, like Carol.

'Dina Dalton. Did you know she was the Midas girl before she became a movie star?'

All Kate knew about Dina Dalton was that at the moment she was regarded as the hottest property in the film industry, and her screen personality had been likened to a cross between Marilyn Monroe and Goldie Hawn—not a bad combination!

'What on earth is the Midas girl?' she queried.

'The hostess on the Midas TV Hour in the States. She introduces the guests and then jokes around with them for a few minutes before they do their acts. Dina's dumb blonde routine became more popular than the celebrities on the show, and she won an Emmy comedy award for it.' Carol named the TV equivalent of an Oscar. 'She's over here to do a new movie, and rumour has it that Scott Jeffreys is putting up most of the money for it. Mind you, as hubby-to-be, why shouldn't he cash in on his asset?'

'That's him with her,' said Mike.

Carol stood on tiptoe to see better. 'Not bad, for a millionaire.' She turned to face Kate and smiled. 'Lucky you, to have such a dishy new boss!'

Kate, tired of hearing about people she could not see, and curious to know what her new employer looked like, caught hold of Mike's arm as he pushed forward through the throng. It pressed all around them as several stars began to move across the foyer, ready to line up to meet the Royal couple who were coming to grace the occasion.

'You can get a good look at them both now,' Carol hissed, and Kate peered through a gap in the crowd to see a tall, willowy girl, with a doll-like face and a mass of golden-blonde hair framing it. 'The colour's natural,' Carol informed her in a disgusted tone. 'She was specially chosen because of their slogan: 'Everything we touch is pure gold.'

In spite of her beauty, it was not the girl who caught and held Kate's attention, but the man at her side: a broad-chested figure with a thatch of thick brown hair.

She caught her breath, and Carol, hearing her, misunderstood the reason.

'Now you can see what I mean about *him*. He's some

hunk of manhood, isn't he? And he's supposed to be crazy about her.'

'Who wouldn't be, unless they were blind?' Trevor added.

Even if it had been to save her life, Kate could not have answered. Dumbly she stared at the smiling couple. There was no mistake about it. The man she had assumed to be a foreman, and whom she had accused of being a thief, was none other than Scott Jeffreys, the new owner of Blakes!

Mortification swamped her. How could he have played such a loathsome trick on her? Of all the mean things to do . . . How he must have laughed to himself when she had used *her* influence to find him a room in his *own* hotel, and then suggested they go Dutch at the Savoy, in case he couldn't afford to pay for her meal!!

'He's—he's younger than I thought he'd be,' she commented, for want of something to say.

'I bet you won't be so quick to hand in your notice, now you've seen him,' Mike chuckled. 'Luckily he's spoken for, or I'd have started to worry!'

Carol and Trevor laughed, and Kate took advantage of it to move into the comparative dimness of the stalls. She wanted to be alone with her thoughts. Scott Jeffreys—the name reverberated in her mind like the chiming of a gong. What a fool he had made of her! Had he intended to keep up the charade when they met for lunch tomorrow? Would he have gone on with the game of insisting she call him darling? Well, she would never know the answer to that, because she had no intention of keeping their date. What kind of man could he be, to flirt with her and ask her out, when he was going to marry another woman? The knowledge of this was more disturbing than anything else, and made it impossible for her to see the rest of his behaviour with the humour with which she would normally have treated it.

'Something wrong?' asked Mike. 'You're sitting there as tense as an overwound spring!'

'Sorry,' she apologised. 'I was thinking of a letter I should have replied to.'

'Forget work—you're here to enjoy yourself.'

Determined not to spoil everyone else's evening, Kate did her best to do as Mike said, and it was past one o'clock when he returned her to her flat. Tiredness make her sleep the moment she put her head on the pillow, but when she awoke to her radio-alarm call, her thoughts immediately flew to Scott Jeffreys.

She would keep him waiting in the Savoy bar, wondering why he had been stood up. No, she wouldn't. She would leave a note with the barman, and make quite sure he knew exactly why she hadn't kept their date. Or could she do something less obvious? Busily she tried to figure out what, discarding one idea after another, until she finally found one that brought a smile of satisfaction to her face. He had said English girls were about as forthcoming as frozen fillets. Well, she would teach him that, true to her word, unless handled carefully, they responded by giving the cold shoulder!

On her way into work she stopped at a supermarket and bought a packet of frozen cod fillets, which she placed in one of the hotel's freezers. At half past twelve she wrapped them in some brown paper and penned a note. It was brief, but to the point.

'I respond to honesty.'

Without bothering to sign her name, she folded it and slipped it into the package, then asked one of the messengers to deliver it to Mr Scott Jeffreys at the Savoy bar.

Lunch with Mike kept further thoughts of Scott Jeffreys at bay, and an appointment with the hotel's insurance broker, regarding a guest's claim, kept her busy until late afternoon, when she made her way back to her office. By now Scott Jeffreys would have received the cod fillets. It was a pity she had not been able to think of some way of being there when he had been presented with them. She would love to have seen his reaction. Anger welled up in her again at the way he had played her for a fool, and she marched through her secretary's room and into her own, stopping short as she saw the man in her thoughts sitting behind her desk.

'Whoever you *did* have lunch with, you certainly took your time,' he said tersely, and stood up.

'I had a business appointment afterwards,' she snapped. 'If you'd taken the trouble to ask my secretary—'

'Do you usually accept invitations and then not go?' he cut in angrily.

'Do you usually pretend to be who you're not?' she retaliated.

'You shouldn't have accepted in the first place if you'd no intention of turning up,' he said, ignoring her question.

'I only decided that after I found out who you were.' As she remembered how she had learned the truth, her anger increased. 'You've certainly got a cheek, being annoyed with *me* after the way *you've* behaved!'

'One of the reasons I asked you to have lunch with me was because I wanted to tell you the truth,' he explained.

'Oh, really?'

'Yes, really,' he said flatly, and then all at once smiled, his wide mouth curving up at the edges, one well-shaped eyebrow raised teasingly. He was impeccably dressed today, she noted, in fine navy hopsack, with blue silk shirt and navy knit tie. For an American he was a conservative dresser, and she wondered if it was his natural inclination, or if he were following a pattern he had set himself—when in Rome . . .

'Surely you can see the funny side of it?' Scott Jeffreys was speaking again. 'You mistook me for the foreman, and I decided to play along with you. What was the harm in that?'

Only the knowledge of his relationship with Dina Dalton enabled Kate to maintain her anger. But it was impossible to tell him her reason, for to have done so would have been tantamount to admitting her jealousy. And that was crazy. How could she be jealous, when she barely knew the man?

'How about starting over again?' He lifted his lids and gave her an intense stare. Even across the width of her desk she could feel the magnetic quality of it, and pressed her feet firmly on the ground in order to keep herself there.

'I'm free on Friday for dinner,' he said.

She had expected him to ask her out that evening, but was careful not to let it show. It did not matter anyway. Her answer would have been the same whatever the day or night.

'I'm afraid I'm not,' she said coolly. 'The only reason I accepted your invitation in the first place was that I didn't want you to think I was a snob. But I have a boy-friend, and he takes up all my free time.'

'I might take your refusal to go out with me now as a form of inverted snobbery,' he suggested slyly, completely ignoring her explanation for refusing. Unlike herself, poaching on someone else's territory did not bother *him* in the least!

'You can take it as you like,' she replied obstinately. 'But I won't change my mind.'

He shrugged resignedly, and moved to the door. 'I hope this episode won't prejudice our working relationship, Kate?'

'I don't see why. One thing has nothing to do with another.'

'In that case, I'll see you in my office at nine-thirty tomorrow morning,' he said, and went out.

As soon as the door in the outer office closed, Janet Williams appeared.

'Why the brush-off?' she asked. 'I couldn't help over-hearing most of it.'

Briefly, Kate explained. 'If he's chasing other girls before the wedding, can you imagine what kind of husband he'll make?' she commented finally.

'It's as well not to get too friendly with him, anyway,' Janet advised. 'With a man as young and attractive as Mr Jeffreys, it can only lead to complications.'

'If our relationship continues the way it's started, I'll probably be given notice by the end of the month!' Kate observed wryly.

But, expecting the worst, she was pleasantly surprised. Certainly Scott Jeffreys was not as easygoing as Roger Blake. Everything had to be done yesterday, giving a sense of urgency which rubbed off on those around him. Moments of calm were rare, and the pace in his office was frenetic. He seemed to find it difficult to relax, and was always on the move, rushing from appointment to appointment, from business breakfasts to business lunches to business dinners. He had irons in several fires other than his hotel group, she learned, and even his weekends were sometimes occupied with meetings that began on Saturday morning and lasted into the evening when, according to Hal Draycott—his right-hand man for the past five years—he would then take everyone to a restaurant for dinner, and on to a nightclub where, with his current girl-friend, he would stay until dawn.

'Sunday is his only official rest day,' Hal told Kate, 'but his Friday night girl always makes herself available for the whole weekend, just in case.'

Which explained his dinner invitation, she thought angrily. Well, one thing was for sure, just because Dina Dalton had returned to the States to tape a TV Special for Midas, there was no way she was prepared to step into her shoes and become Scott Jeffreys' weekend girl-friend.

'It seems a pretty arid existence,' Kate commented aloud. 'Doesn't he have any hobbies or interests outside business?'

'Of course,' Hal said noncommittally. 'But he considers his business to be his main hobby—that's one of the reasons for his success.'

Intensely loyal, Hal obviously did not wish to discuss his employer's personal life other than in general terms, and restraining her curiosity to learn more about him, Kate turned her mind back to business.

The general staff responded to Scott Jeffreys' get-up-and-go attitude with equal fervour, and there was a noticeable tightening up in efficiency. No doubt they were relieved, too, that there had been no drastic innovations. But they were to come, and Kate, as she conducted her employer around the hotel, was one of the first to hear about them. One of her assignments was to acquaint him with the layout, a knowledge he had gained from familiarising himself with the printed plans of Blakes.

Strolling with apparent casualness, he was well aware of the covert glances from passing staff who, at the sight of him, seemed affected with sudden energy. But for the moment, his interest was not in them, but in the physical condition of the hotel, and the alterations he had in mind for it.

A quick scrutiny of the massive pillars in the lobby told him they weren't holding anything up, and could be hollowed out and used as showcases for local shops and department stores, from which a sizeable rental could be demanded. The florist, located in a prime area near the main entrance, also came in for criticism.

'A gift shop would be far more profitable. Our flower trade is negligible, and mainly comes from outside the hotel anyway, so if we can't relocate it, we'll do away with it completely.'

Beneath the main lobby was a large indoor swimming pool, one of the amenities of the hotel that was available to guests free of charge.

'Massage, Sauna, Jacuzzi, Gymnasium, Unisex Hairdresser and Beauty Parlour,' he stated briefly, before moving up to the ground floor again to inspect the restaurants. 'The only thing that comes free of charge in Midas Hotels is water from the taps!'

'The pool's one of the most famous art deco features of the hotel,' Kate said wistfully. 'Syrie Maugham was reputed to have had a hand in the design.'

'Perhaps we'll keep the new complex in that period, then, even use some of the original tiles and panels if they can be removed easily. I do have some sense of tradition, Kate, but as a businessman, I know my sense of profit has to come first.'

They moved up to the ground floor to inspect the restaurants.

'We'll get rid of most of this seating,' Scott Jeffreys commented, as they walked through the busy, cavernous lobby. 'If clients want to sit down, it's more profitable if they do so in one of the bars or restaurants.'

Eliminating some of the existing public area in favour of another half-dozen sales counters—airlines, car rentals, tours, theatre bookings, bureau de change, perfumerie— were other money-spinning ideas, all of which could be undertaken at comparatively little cost.

The same could not be said for his grandiose scheme for building an outsize Edwardian glass conservatory to replace the main restaurant. To be named the Crystal Palace, it would create the illusion of alfresco eating, with lush greenery, banks of flowers, and a waterfall. There would be a barbecue section, where guests could choose their own meat, fish or poultry, creating a further illusion of the outdoors, as would the white wrought-iron furniture with floral printed cushions and matching tablecloths and napkins.

'Every Midas Hotel has a special feature for which it's famous. But unlike the swimming pool here, our show-pieces generate an income, and are wholly practical,' he told Kate, on their return to his office some two hours later. 'What do you think so far of my improvement scheme?'

'I'd prefer to reserve judgment until I see *all* the alterations,' Kate answered tactfully. 'But I'm relieved you're not completely changing the character of the hotel.'

'As I have Mr Blake's penthouse,' he added slyly. 'Every time you come in here, I can read the disapproval on your face!'

He sat down behind his desk—of black ash with black satin aluminium detailing—and made a few notes on a pad before continuing. The Charles Eames chair creaked beneath his weight and his wide shoulders hid the black leather completely.

'The next step will be updating the system of running

the hotel,' he said, as he looked up and indicated that she should take the seat opposite him.

'I suppose that means less personal service and more automation,' said Kate, as she complied.

'Automation spells speed and efficiency, which in turn spells greater profits,' he grunted. 'Old style hospitality is a luxury we can no longer afford.'

'But many of our clients come here solely because of it,' she protested.

'Then they'll have to stay at Claridges or the Connaught in future, if they're not satisfied,' he said incisively. 'When you command a fleet, as I do, you can't run individual ships. Uniformity is the name of the game, however distasteful people like you might find it.'

Taking aim—she suspected unavailingly—Kate said: 'Running a hotel your way lacks warmth and humanity.'

He shrugged. 'It's the way that pays dividends.'

'Financial, perhaps, but not human.'

'I try to take both into account, but I'm in business to make money, Kate, and I have to get my priorities in the right order.'

'We must agree to differ on whether you have, Mr Jeffreys,' Kate answered, undeterred. Feeling she had nothing more to say to him, she began to rise. But he waved her down again, indicating that their meeting was not yet at an end as far as he was concerned.

'I'm pleased with the amount of publicity the hotel's received since the takeover,' he told her, 'You've done an excellent job.'

'Thank you,' she murmured, and unaccountably felt her cheeks redden at his praise.

But he seemed not to notice, and carried on speaking. 'Good enough for me to think you might be able to handle

Dina Dalton's publicity. She's returning to London tomorrow to start work on a new movie, part of which is to be filmed on location in Dublin. No doubt you've heard the rumour that Midas are putting up the money for it?' The question was rhetorical, as he did not wait for her reply. 'She's an extraordinarily talented girl, and is lucky enough to have looks to match. If you've seen her on the screen you'll know what I mean.'

'I have and I do,' Kate acknowledged briefly.

'Normally the studio would handle her publicity themselves, but she had a bust-up with the guy in charge, and refuses to have anything more to do with him. Rather than hire someone I don't know, I thought it might be more sensible to plump for the devil I do!'

'Thanks!' Kate said drily.

He smiled. 'I meant it as a compliment, although I agree, it didn't come out quite that way.'

'You mentioned Dublin. Would I be expected to accompany Miss Dalton there?'

'Would you have any objections?'

Kate shrugged. 'What about my work here?'

'You'll only be away for a few weeks, and unless there's an emergency, I'm sure you'll manage to leave things so that Janet can cope.' He set his hands down on the flat top in front of him. They were big hands, she noticed, with long fingers, the nails short and beautifully manicured.

'You're a pretty efficient young lady,' he said conversationally. '*You* seem able to cope with most things well. That goes for your boy-friend too,' he added.

'Mike, you mean?'

'Do you have more than one in the hotel?'

Kate shook her head, and he smiled. 'I'm sure he'll be pleased to know you're satisfied with him,' she said.

'Are you serious about him?' he asked.

'We see a good deal of each other,' she prevaricated.

'That wasn't the question I asked you,' he said testily.

'I don't see that I need to give a more positive answer, Mr Jeffreys. After all, my personal life is none of your business.'

His eyes glinted. 'Everything about my employees is my business.'

'I'm sorry, but I have to disagree. Unless it interferes with my job, my personal life is my own.'

The glint in his eyes was more pronounced. 'Your job is a particularly demanding one, and it requires a hundred per cent attention. Women in love are notoriously slack.'

'As you've just told me I manage things pretty well, I can't see that that applies to me—in which case, I don't feel your question has any relevance.'

He leaned back in his chair and folded his arms across his chest. It gave him a disarming air of calmness. But to Kate, watching him carefully, he seemed to epitomise a lizard: emotionless and inscrutable, every muscle tensed, ready to pounce when the victim came within striking distance.

'You certainly believe in speaking your mind, don't you?' he observed.

'I thought you didn't like your staff to be intimidated by you?'

'I have no fear of that happening to you,' he said dryly. 'I'm the one likely to end up intimidated!'

'I doubt that, Mr Jeffreys. You're well able to take care of yourself.'

'That depends on my adversary,' he smiled.

'I hope you don't think of *me* as an adversary,' Kate remarked.

'I get the impression you haven't entirely forgiven me

yet—even though I've followed your advice and handled you carefully.' He smiled again, reminding her of their conversation when they had first met. 'You obviously defrost at a very slow rate!'

'Nonsense,' she snapped. 'Of course I've forgiven you. In fact, I haven't thought about it since.'

'How about proving it, then?' he drawled. 'I'm free for lunch today.'

'Sorry, but I already have a date,' she lied swiftly.

'With Mike Wentworth?'

'With a girl friend,' she corrected.

He hesitated, and she wondered if he was going to ask her if she would cancel it. But he didn't. Instead, he changed the subject completely.

'Are you a career girl, Kate?'

Kate ran her tongue over her lower lip. 'What exactly is your definition of a career girl?'

'A woman who prefers to devote herself to her job rather than diversify her energies by having to cope with a husband and children.'

'Some women successfully manage to combine the two,' she pointed out.

'I've not found it so. One or other is bound to suffer.'

'Men have a home and family as well as a job.'

'They're different from women,' he asserted. 'They don't feel guilty when they leave the baby and go to the office, but I've yet to meet a woman who doesn't want to rush home the minute her child starts crying for her.' His glance was quizzical. 'You could go a long way with Midas, if you have the dedication to stay the course.'

'By staying the course, I presume you mean staying single?' He nodded, and she continued. 'I'm not planning marriage in the immediate future, if that's what's concerning you.'

'Good,' he acknowledged smoothly. 'To get to the top, the *company* has to come first.'

'Is that why *you're* still single, Mr Jeffreys?' she ventured.

'I could refuse to answer on the grounds that my personal life has nothing to do with you,' he suggested, unable to resist the jibe, and Kate felt herself redden at this warranted rebuke. 'But I won't.' He leaned forward and clasped his hands together on the blotter in front of him, the long fingers intertwining one with the other. 'The reason I'm not married is quite simple. I've not yet met a woman who could hold my interest on a permanent basis.'

'Does that include Miss Dalton?'

'Dina?' He looked surprised. 'What makes you ask about her?'

Irritated at her impulsiveness, Kate realised there was no way of avoiding a direct answer. 'Rumour has it you're going to marry her,' she said.

'Surely a girl in your line of work knows better than to believe in rumours?' he countered.

A girl in my line of work also knows there's usually no smoke without fire, Kate reflected, but decided *that* thought was best kept to herself.

'Is that why you've refused to go out with me?' Scott Jeffreys was speaking again.

Once again she felt herself redden, and hoped he had not noticed. 'Of course not.' She denied it hotly, and racked her brains for a convincing explanation. 'Part of my job is to liaise between the staff and yourself. If our relationship took a more personal turn, it would make my position untenable.'

'Highly commendable,' he observed dryly. 'Do you always put business before pleasure?'

'Isn't that what *you* advocate?'

Before he could reply, his intercom buzzed, and his secretary's voice informed him of a phone call from Johannesburg.

'Put it through,' he instructed, and nodded in Kate's direction.

Taking this as a sign of dismissal, Kate moved towards the door, Scott Jeffreys, already absorbed in conversation, did not even look up, and she closed it quietly behind her.

Having lied to him about her date, she decided it would be safer not to lunch in the hotel, just in case she bumped into him. Although he usually ate in the private dining-room of his suite when he was not occupied elsewhere, he occasionally liked to surprise the staff by descending on one or other of the restaurants.

Tucking into a mound of fettuccini alla crema in a small trattoria off the Strand, Kate mulled over his offer of promotion, wondering if he had meant it. Scott Jeffreys was a man accustomed to having his own way with women, and might have used it as a ploy to induce her to go out with him. With her usual candour, she admitted that the temptation to accept his invitation had been strong. There must be something in what scientists said about people being attracted to each other because of chemistry. Whatever formula went to make up that particular man, it was certainly potent enough to create havoc inside her. But an affair with him, however exciting, was not what she was looking for.

Having reached the age of twenty-three without succumbing to the easy sexual freedom followed by many of her contemporaries, she had no intentions of submitting to a rugged American who was committed to another woman, and who probably saw her as a last fling before his marriage. It was not a question of prudishness—of which several boy-friends had accused her—but a realisation of her own intensity. When she gave herself to a man, she wanted to give her heart as well as her body. Having been brought up by parents who were devoted to each other, and who had remained faithful throughout their marriage, she appreciated what a real relationship could be between a man and a woman. If this made her an old-fashioned romantic, so be it.

As soon as she returned to her office, she set about the task Scott Jeffreys had assigned her, and set up several interviews and photographic sessions for Dina Dalton—the dates to be confirmed after the girl's arrival the following day.

Although Kate had good contacts in all the media after her two years as Publicity Officer for Blakes, Scott Jeffreys' name opened several doors that would normally have remained closed to her, and confirmed—if indeed she needed any further proof—the power and influence he wielded, even on this side of the Atlantic.

By five-thirty she was reasonably satisfied with her progress, and deciding it was too late to make any more phone calls, and with nothing on her desk that could not be dealt with the following day, prepared to leave the office.

She was halfway out of the door when the intercom connecting her directly with Scott Jeffreys' suite buzzed.

Kate hesitated, debating whether to answer or ignore it. She was going out to dinner with her flatmate and two other girl friends, and had been glad of the opportunity to leave reasonably early. Previous experience had taught her an enquiry from Mr Jeffreys could mean a long delay.

But conscience—and curiosity—got the better of her, and she moved to her desk and flicked the switch down.

'Glad I caught you.' It was Liz Crowther, Scott Jeffreys' secretary, sounding harassed, as usual. 'Mr Jeffreys has to fly to Paris first thing tomorrow morning with Mr Endicott, so he won't be able to meet Miss Dalton's plane. His car and chauffeur are laid on, but he'd like you to deputise for him and make sure she's not bothered by anyone or anything at the airport.'

'I know I'm handling her publicity, but I didn't know that included acting as her nursemaid,' Kate grumbled.

'Sorry, luv—I'm only repeating orders. Mr Jeffreys is tied up in a meeting that looks like going on for half the night, otherwise he'd have told you himself.'

Kate sighed resignedly. 'Accept *my* apologies, Liz—I know it's not your fault. What time is the plane due in?'

'Nine-fifteen. Bradman,' she named the chauffeur who had originally worked for Roger Blake, 'will call for you at seven-forty-five.'

'It doesn't take an hour and a half to get to London Airport from Hampstead,' Kate protested.

'I know, but Mr Jeffreys said to err on the right side in case the plane comes in early. Apparently Miss Dalton occasionally suffers from air-sickness, and has a phobia about being harassed by reporters and fans.'

Bradman was the soul of efficiency, and as Kate had expected, arrived promptly to time. In spite of the early hour, it was not particularly cold, and the sky was bright blue, with just a hint of cloud on the horizon. The road was crowded, but they were driving against the traffic, and arrived at the airport with over half an hour to spare.

Terminal Three was fairly busy, and most of the seats were occupied. Accompanied by the chauffeur, Kate made her way to the flight computer to check the arrival time of Dina Dalton's plane, and was irritated to find its departure from New York had been delayed by an hour, and was not now due to land until ten-thirty.

'It's my fault,' Bradman, a burly, redhaired Welshman, apologised. 'I should have phoned.'

'I'm just as much to blame,' Kate replied. 'I knew there was a baggage handlers' strike, and that often causes delays.'

'Why don't we go over to one of the airport hotels and have some breakfast?' the man suggested. 'I don't know about you, but I only had time for a quick cuppa before I left home.'

'It's as good a way of passing the time as any,' Kate agreed. 'And the food here is pretty dreadful.'

Emerging from the Skyways Hotel an hour and a quarter later, replete after a full English breakfast, they were astonished to find a torrential thunderstorm in progress. The restaurant had been windowless, and completely soundproofed, so they had been quite unaware of the change in weather.

'Luckily I always keep a large umbrella in the boot,' said Bradman, as they turned back on to the motorway. 'I'd hate Miss Dalton to get wet. Mr Jeffreys put me at her disposal when she was in London a few weeks ago, and I can tell you, it doesn't take much to set that young lady off at a tangent!'

'Stars are often temperamental,' Kate agreed.

'One successful film doesn't make her a star in my book,' the chauffeur snorted.

'Perhaps, but she's certainly got the looks of one.'

'And doesn't she know it,' Bradman continued in the same disdainful tone. 'I can't understand what a clever chap like Mr Jeffreys sees in her.'

'Far be it for *me* to tell you,' Kate murmured demurely, 'but if you don't know by now, you never will!'

The chauffeur chuckled. 'As I always say when I want to console my old lady—looks aren't everything!'

It was Kate's turn to smile. 'To some men they are. Perhaps Mr Jeffreys is one of them.'

Hopeful the chauffeur would take up the bait, she was disappointed, for he changed the subject completely.

'It's as well we don't have far to go,' he said. 'We're barely doing fifteen, and I daren't go any faster in this rain.'

'It looks as if you're going to have to go even slower,' Kate replied with concern. 'There's some kind of hold-up ahead.'

'There's been a flash-flood in one of the tunnels leading to the airport,' a policeman controlling the traffic told them, when they drew alongside him some twenty minutes later. 'The drains couldn't cope with the downpour.'

'Any idea how long it's going to take to clear?' Bradman enquired.

The policeman shrugged. 'Half an hour, I'd guess, now the rain's easing off.'

Kate glanced at her watch. It showed ten-thirty. Allowing for the delay caused by the baggage handlers' strike, they probably had about that much time before the actress emerged from Customs.

'I think I'll walk to the Terminal,' said Kate. 'At least if Miss Dalton's one of the first through, I'll be there to explain what's happened.'

Bradman nodded. 'Good idea. I'll get you the umbrella. It's only drizzling now, but it's enough to soak you, just the same.'

Half walking, half running, Kate dashed up the staircase of Terminal Three, and once again scanned the flight computer. She stared, hardly able to believe her eyes.

Flight 842 from New York had touched down exactly to time at nine-fifteen!

'There seems to be something wrong with the computer,' she told one of the girls at the information desk, and went on to explain why.

The hostess smiled apologetically. 'It was wrong earlier on, but we didn't realise it for about five minutes. That must have been about the time you were first here.'

Kate's heart thumped. 'You mean to say it's correct now?'

The girl nodded. 'Were you meeting someone on that flight?'

'Yes—a Miss Dalton—Dina Dalton, the actress,' Kate added. 'Blonde and very pretty.'

A look of recognition enlivened the hostess's face. 'You couldn't miss her. Apart from the looks, I mean. She was mobbed by reporters and fans. I'm one of them,' she confessed with a smile. 'If I hadn't been on duty, I'd have asked for her autograph myself.'

'Damn!' Kate swore softly. 'Is she still here, by any chance, or did she take a taxi?'

'She's waiting in one of the VIP lounges. I'll send a messenger up right away to tell her you're here.'

Kate murmured her thanks. 'My boss is going to be furious with me,' she said, as she waited by the desk for Dina Dalton to appear.

'You have my sympathies,' the hostess smiled. 'She looked fit to be tied. It took twenty minutes before one of the bigwigs rescued her.'

Refusing to be intimidated in advance, Kate fixed a welcoming smile to her face as the actress—white mink coat casually slung over one shoulder—appeared, followed by two stewards wheeling trolleys, piled high with luggage.

Seeing her in close-up, it was still impossible to fault her beauty, though this was slightly marred now by a hardness in the electric-blue eyes. Like Kate, she was wearing a trouser suit, but in softest tan kid that caused Kate to momentarily despise her own sage wool one. Mass-produced Jaeger could not compare with the cut of a model, and this one Kate recognised from the cover of last month's *Vogue*.

'I'm terribly sorry,' Kate began to apologise. 'I was here on time, but the flight computer—'

'You idiot!' the girl bit out furiously, cutting her short. 'Why the hell didn't you double-check with the desk when you saw my plane was late?'

'I didn't think—'

'Minions never do—that's why they're minions!' She eyed Kate coldly. 'Where's the chauffeur?'

'I'm afraid he's stuck in a traffic jam outside the airport. There was a flash-flood caused by the storm, and—'

'You mean to say that after all this hanging around, I'll *still* have to take a cab?' Impatiently, the blonde interrupted once again. 'My God, wait until Scott hears about *this*!'

'I can only apologise again,' Kate murmured, deciding to abandon any further explanatory attempts for the moment. 'I'll go outside and see if he's arrived. With a bit of luck—'

'You'll need *plenty* of it if you want to hang on to your job after this farce,' the blonde stormed. 'Of all the incompetent, stupid—'

Not waiting to hear any more of the girl's recriminations, Kate walked towards the exit, and heaved a sigh of relief as she saw Bradman draw up outside. Strictly illegal, she wondered how he'd managed it.

'Told the bobby on duty I was meeting a Minister,' he grinned cheekily, reading the question on her face. 'Knowing all the traffic had been held up by the storm, he couldn't have been more obliging.'

'The storm may be over outside, but it's still raging in here!' Kate warned.

'Like that, is it?'

'And more!' Swiftly she explained what had happened. 'I only hope Mr Jeffreys is more understanding than she is,' Kate said finally. 'Otherwise we might both be looking for new jobs.'

'Don't worry about Mr Jeffreys,' Bradman soothed. 'Like Mr Blake, he's a fair man, and we'll get a fair hearing.'

The journey back to London was conducted in complete silence by Dina Dalton, who sat on her own at the rear of the limousine, with the partitioning window firmly closed. Bradman, who was normally chatty, also spoke little, perhaps wondering, after encountering the full force of the actress's fury, if he had been overly optimistic about his boss's reaction to the morning's events.

'Is Miss Dalton staying at the hotel?' Kate asked, as they reached Shepherd's Bush.

'Just for the night, I believe. Mr Jeffreys is flying back especially to see her.'

'I suppose when she was last in London he was with her all the time,' Kate remarked casually, wondering if she would have more success pumping the chauffeur about Scott Jeffreys, than previously.

But once again she was disappointed, for Bradman showed a reluctance to gossip—or perhaps had been warned not to.

'I rarely drive Mr Jeffreys outside office hours, so I'm afraid I've no idea who he sees, or where he goes,' the man replied discreetly, and fell silent again until they drew up at the entrance to the hotel.

Charles Granville, the manager, greeted the actress at the door, and with the experience of years, swiftly summed up the situation. Without troubling her to register, he ushered her into the lift.

'No doubt you're tired after the journey,' he murmured with a sympathetic smile. 'So we can dispose of the formalities until you're rested.'

She had been assigned the Royal Suite, which had in its time housed a succession of distinguished guests, including kings, queens and presidents. It was situated on the floor below Scott Jeffreys, and occupied the same area. Furnished elegantly and luxuriously in blue, ivory and gold, in the style of Louis XVI, a large terrace, overlooking the river, led off the main sitting-room and bedroom.

But the actress merely accepted the sumptuous surroundings as her due, and it was the dozen or more gold baskets of hothouse blooms that elicited the first sign of genuine pleasure from her. They were all, the manager explained, from Mr Jeffreys.

He plucked a card from one of them, and handed it to her. 'Mr Jeffreys left instructions for you to read this with your first glass of champagne. It's in the fridge behind the bar,' the man added. 'Krug. He was most explicit regarding your preference.'

'In that case, I'll have some right away,' the blonde smiled. 'And perhaps you could arrange for a plate of smoked salmon and some caviar to go with it. The food on the plane, even in first-class, was inedible, and I'm ravenous!'

'Do you need me for anything else?' asked Kate, as the padded leather doors, decorated with gold crowns, closed silently behind the manager. 'If not . . .'

'Mr Granville seems *most* efficient, and I'm sure he's more than capable of looking after me until Scott arrives.' The girl nodded dismissively, and moved towards the bedroom.

In the circumstances, Kate had not expected profuse thanks, but neither had she expected quite such ungraciousness. Did the actress imagine she had purposely kept her waiting at the airport? Certainly her uncompromising attitude left that impression, and no doubt it was the one she would convey to Scott Jeffreys.

But expecting to be summoned to his office the following morning, Kate was surprised to find he had already returned to Paris on an early plane, and would not be returning to London for several days.

'One night of love to assure her of his undying passion, and back to business—something I suspect he loves far more than any girl friend!' Kate commented to Mike over lunch.

'Fortunately *I* don't.' Mike regarded her tenderly. 'Perhaps that's why I'll never be a tycoon, like Mr Jeffreys.'

'But no doubt you'll make a much better husband. It's the amount of time and effort one puts into a marriage that makes it a success, not the amount of money.'

'For someone like you, perhaps,' he replied. 'But the Dina Daltons of this world want more than a rose-covered cottage in the country and slippers by the fireside!'

'I have a feeling you do as well,' Kate teased. 'The nearest to a cottage you'll ever get is a mews house in Belgravia!'

He smiled. 'I suppose I am a town person—perhaps it's because I never saw the countryside until I was well into my teens. I feel lost when I have too much space around me—insecure, I suppose is the word I'm really looking for.'

But it was more of an emotional insecurity, Kate guessed, than a physical one. Lacking family ties, Mike clung to the city of his birth to give him the roots he lacked.

'But not insecure when it comes to how I feel about you,' he added swiftly, breaking into her thoughts. 'You're far too lovely to be single at twenty-three.'

'I'm far too lovely to be married at twenty-three!'

Fortuitously, the sweet trolley appeared, saving Kate the effort of changing tack herself. She was in no mood for another marriage proposal, and it was becoming increasingly difficult to have a conversation with Mike that did not quickly become too serious or personal.

'I'm going to skip dessert, if you don't mind,' she said, much to his surprise. 'I have a pile of complaints letters to sort through. It's a job I hate, and I've been putting it off for days.'

'There should be an official complaints department. You seem to get all the dirty jobs no one else wants to do,' he answered, looking disgruntled, more at her early departure than her work, she suspected.

'I knew it was part of Public Relations when I took it on, so I can't really grumble. There are some nice aspects to it too,' she added. 'If Miss Dalton is still agreeable to having me work for her after yesterday's fiasco, I might even get some free travel.'

'Really?' He looked interested. 'Where to?'

'Nowhere terribly far or too exciting,' she smiled, as she rose and picked up her shoulder bag. 'Ireland—Dublin,' she answered his question before he could voice it. 'So there's no cause for concern.'

'How long will you be away?'

'I've no idea—and at the moment, it's all very much in the air.'

Rather like her future with Midas, she mused, as she left the dining-room. And that question would not be resolved until Scott Jeffreys' return.

CHAPTER FOUR

To Kate's surprise, Scott Jeffreys did not summon her to his office upon his return. Perhaps in the intervening period Dina Dalton had thought things over and concluded that the mix-up at the airport had been caused by an unavoidable sequence of events. Or more likely, with other, more important things on her mind, she had simply dismissed it as of little consequence. In any event, she had moved out of the hotel, and had sounded perfectly agreeable when Kate telephoned her in the middle of the following week to arrange to see her to discuss her publicity.

'I have some costume fittings in the morning,' the girl told Kate over the telephone, when she suggested they get together the next day. 'So come up and see me any time you like in the afternoon.'

The actress was staying in a rented apartment near the Carlton Towers hotel, and miraculously, Kate found a meter just opposite. The building was a new one, with a video security system. A disembodied voice answered her ring, and in heavily accented English asked who she was. As soon as she stated her name, the entrance door clicked unlocked.

A uniformed maid of Italian or Spanish extraction answered the front door, and ushered her through a small, marble-tiled lobby into a luxuriously furnished lounge. Like the Royal Suite before it, hothouse blooms at a peak of perfection cascaded in colourful profusion from an assortment of vases and containers—no doubt a further sign of Scott Jeffreys' devotion.

Before Kate could seat herself, the woman came back to tell her Miss Dalton would see her in the bedroom.

'She's resting,' the maid said accusingly.

'I was expected,' Kate smiled, and followed her back across the lobby and into a suite. A half-open door gave on to a pale metallic gold bathroom, and the door beside it led into a bedroom that could only be described as sumptuous. A fourposter bed in solid brass predominated, the canopy draped with ethereal curtains in ivory, lined with palest turquoise silk. The thick wool carpet was in ivory too, and the tub chairs and sofa covered in a striking parrot tulip design incorporating the two colours, as well as touches of green and pink. A matching ruched blind was half raised at the window, giving a glimpse of the tops of the trees in the square below.

Dina Dalton herself lay upon shell pink satin sheets—her own, Kate learned later, without which she never travelled—their pillows edged and frilled in lace. Her chiffon negligee was in an almost identical shade, and the soft colouring highlighted her astonishing tumble of golden-blonde hair. It was impossible not to admire her beauty, and to wonder how Scott Jeffreys could ever be bored by it.

'Lovely, isn't it?' Dina drawled, noticing Kate's admiring look. 'Scott managed to get the owner's permission to refurbish this room to my own taste—it's so important to feel at home in one's bedroom, isn't it?'

'What happens when you leave?' Kate asked curiously. 'Will you have to restore it to the way it was originally?'

The girl shrugged indifferently. 'I never bother with details. Scott arranged it all. When we're together, he likes my mind free to concentrate on him alone.' She snuggled back against the cushions. 'Make yourself comfortable,'

she said, and waited until Kate had settled on a chair close
to the bed. 'Now tell me all the marvellous things you've
planned for me. I'd have preferred to use Frank Martin,'
she named one of the best known public relations firms,
'but Scott assured me you're excellent at your job.'

Concisely, Kate recounted the publicity she had
arranged—and what she was still hoping for—in order to
promote Dina's appearance in her second movie, conclud-
ing with the promise of a prestigious magazine to feature
her on their front cover.

'You've obviously got friends in high places,' the girl
commented, looking impressed for the first time.

'Not really. I just promised them a full page advert in
next month's edition.'

'Oh well. Public relations is all tit for tat, isn't it?'

'I wouldn't exactly say that,' Kate replied with a smile.
'But sometimes a good turn doesn't go amiss.'

'I'd like to appear on the Ronnie Peters Hour as well,'
said Dina, naming the longest running, and most popular,
chat show on TV.

'I'm afraid that's one person I have no influence with,
and he's an extremely difficult man to approach.'

'Get Scott to ask him, then. He's met him a couple of
times in the States,' the blonde instructed imperiously.

'It would be a waste of time,' Kate said, knowing this
from past experience. 'Mr Peters isn't the sort to do
favours, even for close friends.'

'We'll see about that.' A scarlet-tipped hand lifted up
the telephone receiver. She dialled quickly, without paus-
ing to think of the number, and her face softened into
gentleness as she spoke. 'Scott, sweetheart, I have Kate
here with me, and I've just told her I want to appear on
the Ronnie Peters Hour. She says it's impossible, but
I told her that you could easily fix it for me. She said

even you wouldn't be able to do it, but . . . Darling, how you do spoil me!' China blue eyes slid to Kate, and the receiver was held out. 'He wants to speak to you.'

Kate took the telephone, and listened quietly as Scott Jeffreys' disembodied voice asked: 'What the hell are you arguing with her for?'

'There's no point in promising the impossible, Mr Jeffreys,' she answered coldly.

'Impossible for you, perhaps,' he said curtly. 'Now agree to whatever she wants, and report back to me if there's anything else you think you can't deliver.'

'Whatever you say, Mr Jeffreys,' she said sweetly, and restraining the urge to bang down the receiver and show her true feelings, set it gently back on the cradle.

'I told you Scott would fix it. He hates to refuse me anything,' Dina said triumphantly, glancing at the silver-framed photograph of him resting on the bedside table. Her expression was languid, as though she was re-membering other times with him. It made his presence in the room almost tangible—and Kate looked at the king-size bed and then hastily stood up.

'I think we've discussed all the points for now, Miss Dalton. I'll have an itinerary typed out for you, and let you have it by tomorrow.'

'How about a drink before you go—coffee, or something stronger if you prefer?'

'Sorry, I haven't time.'

'A cigarette, then?' Dina bent towards the bedside table. Her breasts, large and full for someone so slender, were revealed as she did so, and she straightened without embarrassment and pulled her wrap more closely around her. 'Maybe the pack is on the dressing table. Have a look for me, will you?'

Kate went over to the ivory and gold lacquered table, with its array of make-up jars and scent bottles.

'There aren't any cigarettes here,' she said.

'Try the top drawer. Scott's trying to make me give them up, and he may have hidden them there last night.'

Kate did as instructed and found a box of filter-tips. She took it out, and the gold Cartier lighter lying beside it. As she picked it up she noticed an inscription, punched out in tiny diamonds on the front. 'From S to D. May all our days be golden.'

Illogically, the intimacy of the wording irritated her, and it took some effort to force a casual smile to her lips as she handed it to the other girl.

But Dina was observant enough to notice her reaction. 'Beautiful, isn't it? Scott gave it to me when I agreed to give up my modelling career and become the Midas girl.' She proffered the cigarettes to Kate, who shook her head.

'I don't, thank you.'

'Wise girl. Still, they're better than liquor, I suppose. At least they don't put on weight and ruin your looks.'

They just give you lung cancer instead, Kate thought to herself, but said aloud:

'I don't drink either.'

'I wasn't suggesting you did, darling,' the actress smiled, but the vivid blue eyes remained hard, contradicting her words.

'I really must go,' Kate said. 'I've masses to do at the office. I can see myself out, thank you,' she added, as the girl's hand reached for the bell to summon the maid.

Relieved to escape the oppressive atmosphere of the apartment, Kate drew a deep breath of fresh air as she reached the front steps of the block. Obviously Scott Jeffreys' relationship with Dina Dalton was an intimate one. Why else would his photograph have been at her bedside? It was obvious too that he had spent the previous night with her. Not that that was surprising. After all, they were having a love-affair. But love—or at least her interpretation of the word—was an emotion she found difficult to attribute to either of the people concerned. It certainly did not preclude Scott Jeffreys' chasing after other women, and as for the actress, she was more likely to see a man as a cushion of security, or as an answer to a purely physical need. Yet it had been rumoured they were to marry, and Kate remembered that though Scott Jeffreys had looked surprised when she had suggested it, he had not actually denied it.

In the office again, she dictated a memorandum to Janet relating to the actress's publicity, and was about to go down to the third floor to speak to the housekeeper about some missing linen—a query that should have been dealt with by the head housekeeper, but one of the many that somehow found its way to her desk—when the buzzer connecting her intercom directly with Scott Jeffreys, sounded.

'Come in and see me right away,' he ordered tersely.

Hurriedly she made her way along the corridor to his suite, where his secretary's sympathetic smile warned her of her employer's mood.

'Sit down,' he ordered, and waited for her to comply before continuing. 'Having managed to talk Dina into keeping you on after the fiasco at the airport, I didn't think I needed to tell you beforehand to handle her with kid gloves,' he said without preamble. 'She was on the phone complaining about you the minute you left her.'

So the girl had neither forgiven nor forgotten. But it seemed that Scott Jeffreys valued her sufficiently to ignore his girl-friend's complaints. For some reason Kate found the knowledge comforting.

'I don't know why, Mr Jeffreys,' she answered with surprise. 'Other than my telling her I couldn't guarantee her an appearance on the Ronnie Peters show, she appeared to be quite happy with things.'

'That one slip was enough to set her wondering if she was missing out on anything else, through not being handled by a professional.'

'Although PR is only part of my job here, I consider myself to *be* professional,' Kate answered stiffly, resenting the implication. 'And in the two years since I started, I haven't had any other complaints.'

'I didn't say I was complaining.' His tone was conciliatory. 'But with twenty million dollars of Midas's money invested in the success of this movie, my aim is to keep Dina happy. That means within reason, whatever Dina wants, Dina gets.'

Including you? she wondered, but thought better of voicing the question aloud.

'I can't perform miracles, I'm afraid,' she replied instead.

'Luckily I can, though. Ronnie Peters has agreed to devote the whole of one of his shows to Dina—you're to phone him on Monday, and he'll let you have the date.'

'You must let me know the secret of your success,' said Kate drily. 'I was under the impression he never did favours for *anyone*.'

Scott Jeffreys' mouth tilted at one corner. 'He doesn't, unless they've done one for him first!'

'And you have?'

He nodded. 'I anticipated he might be useful to me at some time or other, so I tipped him some shares the last time I saw him in New York.'

'Lucky they went up, then!'

'Luck had nothing to do with it,' Scott Jeffreys stated matter-of-factly. 'I owned the company whose shares I tipped.'

Kate could not help smiling. 'Is everything you touch guaranteed to turn to gold, Mr Jeffreys?'

'I didn't name my company Midas by accident, Kate,' he smiled back. 'Though I'm neither arrogant nor conceited enough to think luck hasn't played some part in my success,' he added modestly. 'I was fortunate enough to be in the right place at the right time at the start of my career.'

'When the hotel you were working for was on the verge of bankruptcy, you mean?'

'Yes. If that hadn't happened, it would have taken me several years longer to get where I am now. But I would have got there just the same—of that I have no doubt,' he said confidently, but with a total lack of conceit.

'Not many people of your age would have had the nerve to lay their careers on the line, the way you did. After all, if things had gone wrong . . .'

He looked whimsical. 'True, but I'm not a gambler, Kate. I didn't approach the hotel's bankers on a whim. I spent weeks beforehand weighing the odds on success, and calculating what needed to be done, and how long it would take to do it. As things turned out, we were in profit six months before the date I predicted.'

'And from then on, as they say, you've never looked back.'

'We're the second largest hotel group in the States,' he stated satisfactorily. 'My ambition is to be number one.'

'Will you be contented then, or will you want to go on to be the largest in the world?'

'Do I detect a note of disapproval?' he asked defensively.

Kate shook her head. 'Not at all. I'm just curious to know why you should want to go on. Is it money, power—'

'Certainly not money. I'm not acquisitive in the financial sense,' he asserted positively, 'although I won't pretend I don't enjoy the advantages it buys. But once one has enough, it ceases to be a motivation.'

'How much is enough?' Kate asked. 'For one it might be a million, another a hundred million.'

'I guess to me enough was when I ceased to know exactly how much I was worth,' he smiled. 'So to answer your question, I guess if I were to be perfectly honest, I'd admit it was power that motivated me—although I prefer to see it as a sense of satisfaction. Satisfaction in reaching the pinnacle—and knowing there's no way you or anyone else can climb any higher.'

'At the rate you're going, you'll probably achieve your aim by the time you're forty,' Kate commented. 'What will you do then? Retire?'

'Heavens, no! I'd die of boredom.'

'Doesn't the lotus life appeal to you?'

'Only in small doses. I come from the kind of background where indolence was regarded as something sinful—and because of it I've never been able to quite shake off a feeling of guilt when I've indulged in a long holiday. You may not believe me, but I even feel guilty if I get up much later than seven-thirty!'

Kate laughed. 'Boarding school gave me a similar hang-up, so I can sympathise.'

'Fortunately I can get by on very little sleep,' he went on conversationally. 'Four or five hours. And like Winston Churchill, I'm able to catnap at will—a few minutes of unconsciousness and I'm completely recharged.'

'What a marvellous knack—particularly for someone like yourself who travels so much.'

'Yes—I guess I'm fortunate. Time changes rarely affect me—although I was pretty done in the first time we met,' he added with a smile of remembrance. 'But that was because I flew over with my crew, and they're not the quietest or most abstemious bunch of guys! I'd hate to tell you how many bottles of whisky they got through on the journey over.'

'Talking of the first time we met, I'd like to ask you something about it.' He nodded, and Kate continued, 'Why on earth were you dressed in that boiler suit?'

'How I wish I hadn't been! Then you wouldn't have mistaken me for the foreman, and we might have started on a rather better footing.' He sighed regretfully. 'But to answer your question, I knocked over a pot of paint, and it soaked the clothes I was wearing. I was staying at the Connaught at the time, if you remember, and rather than send over for another suit, I borrowed a spare pair of overalls from one of my men.' His eyes widened, making her aware of the greenish-gold flecks in them. 'It's a pity you found out who I was before you went out with me. I'm quite irresistible once you get to know me!'

'I may be small in stature, Mr Jeffreys, but I'm not short on will-power!'

He chuckled. 'I'm ready to put it to the test any time you say.'

'Are you always this persistent?' Kate asked crossly.

'Only when I want something badly enough.' He moved his eyes indolently over her face, as if he were making an inventory of each feature. 'Being the boss's girl-friend would put you in a very advantageous position.'

'It's the other position I don't fancy,' she answered crisply. 'I have no desire to further my career via your bedroom.'

'No one would ever get to my boardroom because of their bedroom abilities,' he assured her smoothly. 'But you're bright as well as beautiful, Kate, and if you make it, it will be because you've earned it, fair and square.'

'Flattery will get you absolutely nowhere, Mr Jeffreys.'

'Don't you believe it!' he countered. 'And given time, I'll prove it to you.'

'Time is a commodity you value highly, so don't bother wasting any more on me,' she answered dulcetly. 'Other than to let me know what you want to do about Miss Dalton's publicity, that is. If you remember, *that* was the reason you asked me in here.'

Defiantly she looked at him, expecting him to show signs of anger. But because he was Scott Jeffreys he did the unexpected, and throwing back his head gave a full throaty laugh.

'If you can stand up to me, I guess you're capable of handling Dina and her tantrums. But for heaven's sake keep her sweet, even if it means telling a few white lies.'

'If I have any difficulty on *that* score, I'm sure you'll be able to advise me!'

'Now what the hell is that supposed to mean?' he asked belligerently. 'You're always—'

But Kate never heard the rest of his reply. A discreet knock at the door heralding the entrance of his secretary halted him in mid-sentence.

'The coffee you asked for, Mr Jeffreys,' the woman said, placing a tray in front of him.

'It's taken so long, I thought you'd forgotten.'

'I'm sorry, but I hadn't realised we were out of coffee. I had to send downstairs for some more,' she explained.

'You may as well bring your notebook in here now, Liz,' Scott told her. 'I want to get off a couple of letters before you go, and my business with Kate is finished—for the moment, anyway,' he added, his expression serious. But the quirk of his mouth as he glanced in her direction told Kate Liz Crowther's entrance only meant a temporary respite. Scott Jeffreys was not a man to give up until the battle was won.

The trouble was, she thought as she made her way down to the third floor to speak to the housekeeper, she was far too aware of him for her own peace of mind, and because of it, she was not sure what she should do if he persisted in his attentions to her. Short of leaving, what more could she do? And that would be childish and stupid in the extreme. She enjoyed her work, and found it stimulating, and it would not be easy to find another job with the same amount of responsibility and independence. In many ways, she was more or less her own boss, and it was a freedom she appreciated.

It was gone seven before she left the hotel. It had been a long day and she was tired. It was a pity she was seeing Mike tonight. She toyed with the idea of calling him and saying she was not feeling well, but then decided it was better to go out with him than sit at home worrying about how to handle Scott Jeffreys.

'You've certainly landed yourself a headache,' Mike commented sympathetically, after Kate had recounted her meeting with Dina Dalton, and a slightly edited version of her subsequent one with Scott Jeffreys. 'She sounds like a prize bitch. Why don't you refuse to do her PR? After all, it's not as if she's connected with the hotel.'

'But she is tied in with Midas—and that's who we all work for now—not just Blakes,' Kate pointed out practically.

'True,' he conceded with a shrug. 'But PR isn't meant

to be your sole occupation. What about your other duties?'

'Hal Draycott handles most of the personal work I used to do for Mr Blake,' Kate explained. 'And as I enjoy the promotional side best, I don't really mind.'

'So you're not privy to the great man's secrets?' Mike teased, but with a hidden edge to his words that made her give him a curious look. 'There are rumours going around of a theft—on quite a grand scale,' he explained. 'I was hoping to get the lowdown from you. If I could find out what section it's in, and expose the culprits before Mr Jeffreys, it would prove how on the ball I am.'

Kate showed no surprise at Mike's revelation. Corruption was one of the hazards of the hotel trade, and there was a multiplicity of ways in which dishonest employees could steal from their employers, particularly in the bar and restaurant division, where it was not easy to detect. Privately purchased wine and other kinds of liquor could be introduced so that inventory checks wouldn't show any shortages, but the proceeds—and hefty profits—would be pocketed by the staff concerned. A bartender could also pour short measures to obtain a few extra drinks from each bottle used, as well as failing to ring up every sale. He could then keep the proceeds from both for himself. With four bars and an equal number of restaurants at Blakes, it could add up to a considerable amount of money.

'I know there's a file on it,' Mike was speaking again, 'and if I could get a look at it . . .'

Kate frowned. 'Mr Jeffreys did send one down to me a couple of weeks ago. It was marked confidential, and he told me to keep it under lock and key in my office safe—he had the other copy in his. Mr Blake used to do that sometimes too, as an extra security precaution.'

'I don't suppose—' Mike began.

'You don't suppose right,' Kate cut him short. 'In my book, confidential means *confidential*!'

He knew from the look on her face he had said the wrong thing, but he was too clever to apologise.

'Pity,' he said casually. 'It might have helped my promotion prospects. I need it to keep you in the manner to which you're accustomed.'

'I should think you could do that already!' she smiled.

He gave her an intent look. 'I wish you'd taken my proposals more seriously. You know you're the only girl I date.'

'That's not my fault,' she answered. 'I've told you often enough I don't mind if you take out other girls.'

'When you've found what you want, why look elsewhere?'

'Because the feeling has to be mutual.'

'Think about it,' urged Mike. 'Perhaps it is.'

'If I were in love with you I wouldn't have to think about it. I'd be aware of it.'

'You haven't let yourself try.'

'It isn't something you can decide to do. It happens whether you want it or not.'

He looked at her quizzically. 'You sound as if you're talking from experience.'

'Not really. But I'm sure when I do meet the right man, I'll know at once.'

'You mean a flash of lightning, and all that rot.'

'And I thought you were a romantic!' she teased.

He reddened. 'I've grown to love you, Kate, and that's far more lasting than a flash of lightning.'

'My parents met in Italy and got engaged after one day

together and their marriage has lasted for twenty-five years, so far!' Kate said. 'So flashes of lightning don't necessarily end in thunderstorms!'

'Perhaps my being an orphan has something to do with your refusal,' he persisted doggedly. 'Some people—'

'Of course it hasn't,' she reassured him truthfully. 'I've never given it a second thought. Anyway, if my married friends are anything to go by, being an orphan can be something of an asset. Most of their arguments seem to be about their respective families!'

Outside the door of her flat, Mike pulled her into his arms. His kiss was fierce as always, and though she did not find it distasteful, she could not abandon herself to it. She wished she could close her mind and feel only with her senses, but though she tried, she became even more selfconscious, and after a moment, pushed against him with her hands.

He released her immediately, though there was a brooding look in his eyes that told her he was far from pleased.

'Saturday, as usual?' he asked.

'Sorry, Mike, but I'm going home for the weekend. It's a couple of months since I've seen my parents, and they've been complaining about it.'

'Who can blame them for missing you,' he smiled warmly. 'See you on Monday.'

His comment made Kate feel the more guilty for lying. Well, perhaps she would visit her parents, after all. Just in case Mike decided to check up on her. If only they didn't work under the same roof, how much easier it would be. But coming into almost daily contact made ending their relationship that much more difficult. And it wasn't as if she didn't like him. The trouble was, things had now reached the stage when liking was not enough. Unless she was prepared to go a step further, and commit herself in some way, she would have to make a clean break, and refuse to date him any more.

CHAPTER FIVE

THE following morning was a busy one, with her weekly press conference held in the main ballroom. It mainly concerned interesting or famous people visiting the hotel, and most of the questions fired at her were routine. A great deal of the coverage they finally received in the newspapers could have been obtained by a press handout, without the expense of canapés and drinks. But it was essential to maintain the goodwill of the reporters, for there were times—like now with Dina Dalton—when she needed them for greater coverage.

At noon she made her way back to her office, but had difficulty entering it, for the corridor was blocked by several men wheeling large boxes on a trolley into the accounts department opposite.

'What's going on?' Kate asked Harry Adams, the credit manager, who was at the door watching the operation.

'It's our new computer system,' he explained. 'All the hotel's accounts—rooms, restaurants, bars—will be fed into it in future.'

'I suppose you'll be going on a computer course to learn how to use it?' Kate smiled sympathetically, remembering how complicated she had found her word processor.

The plump, grey-haired man shook his head. 'You can't teach an old dog new tricks,' he said sadly. 'Mr Jeffreys has taken on a computer expert to reorganise the department, and he'll be employing new staff to help him.'

'You—you mean you've been fired?'

'Retired is the word Mr Jeffreys used—but it amounts to the same thing, doesn't it?'

The elderly man sounded bitter, and Kate did not blame him. He had been a faithful servant of Blakes for thirty years, and his section was one of the most efficient. There was little that the credit manager's shrewd, encyclopaedic mind missed, a fact which in the past had saved the hotel thousands of pounds in bad debts.

'I don't know what to say.'

Harry Adams smiled ruefully. 'There isn't anything to say, Kate. I'm not the only one who's being given the push, and if Mr Jeffreys intends to automate us completely, like his other hotels, there'll be at least a couple of hundred or so others retired or made redundant.'

'We'll fight it,' Kate said fiercely. 'He promised—'

'If you remember what he said when it was first announced that he had bought Blakes, you'd have realised, as I did, that his promises didn't mean a thing. "I'm in business to make money",' Harry Adams quoted. '"Not a philanthropist with an urge to preserve ancient monuments".' He shook his head sadly. 'I suppose that's what we old-timers really are—ancient monuments.'

'He's right of course,' Janet Williams said practically, when Kate finally reached her own office, and recounted what was happening. 'Automation is a natural progression, and should have happened years ago. At least that way most of the firings would have been avoided, and happened by natural wastage instead. The kitchens are next on the list, I hear, and the main restaurant's being turned into a round-the-clock coffee shop.'

'So that's why Mr Jeffreys showed such an interest in it. I thought he just intended to refurbish it so he could squeeze in more tables.'

'The French Room and the Club House are being

retained as is, and the Crystal Palace will become the main restaurant.'

'How do you know all this?' Kate asked curiously.

'Bill Sanderson,' Janet explained, naming the head doorman, who always knew everything that was going on in the hotel—sometimes before it happened! 'We usually have a drink together after work.'

'Romance blooming?' Kate questioned. Janet had been a widow for many years, and she knew that Bill's wife had died the previous summer.

'Perhaps.' The older woman reddened. 'His wife and I were best friends. She was a floor housekeeper here—you know?' Kate nodded, and Janet continued. 'Bill's lonely. Unfortunately, he and Madge had no kids.'

'Well, at least his job's safe—unless Mr Jeffreys gets a robot, there's no way he can be replaced!'

If there had been a noticeable tightening of efficiency before rumours of the intended alterations started circulating, now there was an even greater flurry of activity. No one felt secure any longer, whatever their job, for they could see, as heads started to roll, that the executioner was merciless. Young and old alike were given notice, though to be fair to Scott Jeffreys, the severance pay he offered to the senior staff was more than generous. Their pensions too were being honoured in full. But nothing could compensate for the loss of their jobs, as for many, being fired after a lifetime's service, also meant a loss of dignity. Men who the previous day had walked with a spring in their step now looked tired and old. It was heartbreaking, but of course made sound business sense, and to Scott Jeffreys and Midas's shareholders, no doubt, that was all that mattered.

It was not until the end of the week that Kate came face to face with the man responsible for all of the misery, and when she did, she found it an effort to be civil to him.

'Mr Jeffreys wants to see you,' Janet Armstrong rushed into her office.

Kate leaned back in her chair. 'Oh, does he?'

'Now,' Janet insisted. 'He's waiting outside.'

'Well, let him wait,' said Kate, wondering what had precipitated the mountain coming to Mahomet. 'I'm busy.'

But her secretary ignored her instructions, and went to the door and held it open.

'*Do* come in, Mr Jeffreys.'

He breezed into the room and stopped in front of Kate's desk.

'I just dropped by to commend you on the way you've smoothed Dina's ruffled feathers. Your phone call telling her you'd arranged a spot on the "Today in Town" show did the trick. I only hope we don't have to pay for it with a series of commercials, though. This tit-for-tat business could become expensive!'

Kate knew he was teasing her about the full-page advert she had promised the magazine who were featuring the actress on their front cover, but she was in no mood to respond lightheartedly.

'It won't cost you a penny, Mr Jeffreys,' she said, tightlipped. 'A friend of mine is an assistant producer on the show, and she arranged it as a favour.'

'There's no need to look so grim. I was only teasing,' he assured her. 'Frankly, I wouldn't have minded whatever the cost. It's Dina's happiness that's important.'

'There's no need to remind me,' Kate answered coolly. 'I'm well aware of it.'

His mouth tightened. 'We're not starting *that* again, are we?'

'What again?' she asked with deliberate innocence.

'Forget it.' His gaze moved slowly over her face. 'You look tired, Kate.'

Automatically she put up a hand to smooth her hair and he caught hold of it in a surprisingly gentle clasp and pushed it down on the desk. 'Your hair is fine, and so is your make-up.'

'When most men say a woman looks tired, they mean she looks a mess!'

'I'm not most men, and I doubt you could ever look a mess,' he replied. 'If I say tired, I mean exactly that. It's in your eyes and the set of your mouth. What's the cause? Devotion to duty, or too many late nights?'

'Devotion to duty on behalf of your protégée,' Kate snapped. 'She's on the phone to me three times a day, and about the same at home in the evenings.'

'Perhaps you'd like to be relieved of the duty?'

'I haven't asked you to, Mr Jeffreys.' Her voice rose and with an effort she lowered it. 'Don't put words into my mouth.'

'Why don't you call me Scott?' he suggested. 'It's so much friendlier. All my senior staff in the States do.'

'*This* isn't the States, *Mr* Jeffreys, and I prefer to do things the *British* way.'

The smile left his face, and his lower lip jutted forward belligerently. 'What an irritating girl you are!'

'If you find me irritating, you're always at liberty to fire me,' she said frostily.

'Now you're putting words into *my* mouth!' he smiled. 'I came here to praise you, not quarrel with you.'

'Well, your mission's accomplished.' She stood up, and moved past him to the door. 'I don't want to keep you—I know what a busy man you are.'

In three strides his long legs had crossed the room and

he was in front of her, pale beneath his tan, his eyes as hard as stones.

'When I'm ready to go, I'll leave,' he bit out furiously. '*I'm* the one who does the dismissing around here, not you.'

'I'm well aware of *that*, Mr Jeffreys,' she said nastily.

'So that's what this is all about?' His anger had gone as quickly as it had come and he folded his arms across his chest and looked at her. 'You're annoyed with me because of the redundancies.'

'Only because you lied, and lulled people into a false sense of security.'

'I never made any definite promises—only an idiot would have done that. It was obvious at a glance that Blakes was overstaffed. And you really didn't think I was going to take over and leave things exactly as they were, did you?' He rocked slightly on his feet. 'The reason Roger Blake sold this hotel to me was that he couldn't make it pay as it was, and the only way to turn things around—without actually knocking the place down—is to introduce new revenue sources and modernise and overhaul some of the existing ones. Initially, there are bound to be some job losses.'

'Some!' Kate expostulated bitterly. 'There'll be a couple of hundred.'

'Considering the size of the work-force, that's small, I assure you,' he said, unperturbed by her criticism. 'I'm sorry, Kate, but I'm a businessman, out to make a profit, and I'm not ashamed of it. I live in a capitalistic society because I believe in the freedom of the individual. I assume you do too. So why condemn me when I'm only abiding by the rules?'

His argument was logical, and Kate knew it. Perhaps if she hadn't regarded so many of those losing their jobs as her friends, she would not have taken the redundancies to heart in the same way. After all, there was not a business in the country—including her own father's—that could afford to keep superfluous staff. And it had to be remembered that Scott Jeffreys had attempted to soften the blow by giving unusually generous severance pay. This showed that however profit-motivated the exterior shell, a social conscience of sorts lurked beneath.

Aware that apologies for her ill-humour were in order she said stiffly: 'You—you're quite right, of course, Mr Jeffreys. I'm afraid I was letting my heart rule my head.'

'With that colour hair, I suppose it's only natural!' he smiled. 'Or is it?' he added quizzically.

'Is what?' she cross-questioned, puzzled.

'Your hair.' He smiled again. 'Is it natural?'

'Inherited from my father,' she told him briefly.

He put his hands into the pockets of his trousers and the material tightened across his hips, bringing to attention the lean line of them and the tautness of his thigh muscles.

'Your looks too?'

'No, just the hair and temper!'

His next words told Kate he had taken her admission as removing the last vestiges of antagonism towards him.

'Well, Miss Spitfire, now we're friends again, how about having dinner with me tonight? A business one, of course,' he added hastily. 'I thought we'd discuss your future with the company.'

'We can do that just as well here, Mr Jeffreys,' said Kate, not believing him for a moment. 'Frankly, I'd prefer it.'

'But I wouldn't—anyway, I haven't time.' He glanced at the thin sliver of platinum on his wrist. 'I should have been at a meeting ten minutes ago, and I'm a stickler for promptness.' He paused, fingers on the door-handle. 'Well?'

Hurriedly she racked her brain for an excuse. 'I—I can't. I'm washing my hair.'

'And brushing me off at the same time!' He shook his head. 'Really, Kate, considering how intelligent you are, that really is the tritest excuse of the year!' He leaned towards her and tweaked a copper-coloured strand. 'I told you earlier on there was nothing wrong with it. But if you insist there is, then leave early and wash it. I'll pick you up at eight. Dress up if you like—I'll book at the Gavroche.' He caught hold of her arm. 'I'm giving an order, so you can appease your conscience by telling yourself you're not going out with your boss because you want to, but because you have no choice!'

The door closed behind him, and Kate was left to gather her wits. She was illogically glad he had ignored her refusal and forced her to do as he wanted, and ignoring Janet's teasing at her capitulation, followed his instructions, and left work early to wash her hair. Having agreed to go out with him, she intended to look her best.

'I thought you were driving down to your parents' this evening?' Lucy, her flatmate, looked surprised to find Kate in the bath at seven, when she arrived home.

'I'm going in the morning instead,' said Kate, and proceeded to explain why.

'I knew you wouldn't be able to resist temptation for long,' Lucy chuckled. 'You don't expect me to swallow that guff about it being a business dinner, do you? You fancy him, Kate. Why not be honest enough to admit it?'

'I do admit it—and that's one of the reasons I've not wanted to go out with him. He'd be easy to fall for, and I don't want to complicate my life.'

'He might fall for you too,' her friend replied.

'But not in a way that matters. Scott Jeffreys is more interested in business than love and marriage.'

'Love and marriage!' Lucy, a willowy brunette, repeated scornfully. 'You're an incurable romantic, Kate. If you like him, and all the other ingredients are right, there's no need to look further.'

'I don't know that I do like him—that's another reason I've refused to date him.'

'Well, there's only one way to find out, and thank heavens you've had the sense to realise it!'

It was easy for Lucy to talk. She had no compunction sleeping with *her* boss—who was married—or any man who took her fancy, including the clients who came into the showroom where she worked as a fashion model.

'Being promiscuous isn't a sin,' Lucy went on, cutting across her thoughts. 'Not unless you're married, that is.'

'Now who's being old-fashioned?' Kate teased, and pulled the plug out of the bath.

'Don't you see the best way of ensuring faithfulness after marriage is by having lots of affairs beforehand?' Her friend handed Kate her towelling robe. 'Otherwise you'll always be wondering what you've been missing.'

Kate smiled. 'On the other hand, if you don't know what you've missed, it might make you more content with what you have.'

Conceding the point, Lucy commandeered the bathroom while Kate went into her room to dress.

Surveying her wardrobe, she sighed. All afternoon she had thought about what she was going to wear, putting off the final decision until this moment. Deep down, though, she had known all along it would be the little black dress. Little was an apt description, she reflected as she put it on, though the word described the briefness of the material rather than the price. It was the most expensive and daring dress she had ever possessed and she had bought it in a fit of bravado while out shopping with Lucy.

'You'll never put it on your back,' her friend had smiled. 'You just want to prove a point.'

Well, she was proving Lucy wrong now. The skilful cut of the silk jersey made the material cling provocatively to every curve of her body, and the starkness of the colour turned her skin to marble and her hair to flame. Her eyes, skilfully shaded with mascara, glowed like luminous green pools, their limpid depths innocent, their slanting shape enticing. Around her throat she wore a thin gold chain with a diamond heart, that with matching earrings had been a twenty first birthday present from her parents.

'He's here, Kate,' Lucy bounded in excitedly. 'He's just rung the bell.'

'Oh, lord—I'm not quite ready! Would you mind entertaining him for a few minutes?'

'Only a girl as innocent as you would trust her best friend with a dishy millionaire!'

Before Kate could think of a suitable retort, the bell rang again, and Lucy hurried to answer it. Kate turned back to the mirror and hastily finished her make-up, then ran a final comb through her hair. It rippled to her shoulders like a heavy fall of satin, and instead of curling under as usual, curled upwards in delicate fronds as it touched her shoulders. She put a hand to her throat, aware of the bare expanse of skin she was showing. The bodice of her dress was designed to be worn braless, and she turned sideways to reassure herself that she did not look shapeless. No, that was a word that definitely could not be applied to her. She briefly touched one full breast with her hand, then with a nervous sigh picked up a black velvet cape, lined in emerald satin, and went into the lounge.

Scott Jeffreys stared at her in silence as she came in, then gave a slight smile and went on talking to Lucy, who was telling him about her summer holiday in Florida. Kate wondered if he was bored, but he was listening with apparent interest, asking the right questions, and seeming to agree with her comments and criticisms.

'I have to go,' she said at last, somewhat reluctantly taking the hint when Kate went to the trolley and offered them both a drink.

But Scott Jeffreys asked for a whisky, and he raised his glass to Kate before he drank.

'Nothing for you?' he asked.

'If we're going to discuss business, it's better if I keep a clear head.'

He raised one well-shaped eyebrow and smiled. 'You don't look as if you're dressed *just* to discuss business. You're quite astonishingly beautiful, Kate,' he said softly. 'But I expect you've been told that any number of times before.'

There was no doubting his sincerity, and her heart thumped hard against her ribs. She did not want him to compliment her like this, nor did she want to be so aware of him. Yet she had done her best to make sure he was aware of her, she admitted, with her usual honesty, and was suddenly overcome with embarrassment.

It was a sensation that was new to her, for only with this dynamic and intriguing man was she so painfully aware of her looks that she became selfconscious.

'No girl ever gets bored being told she's beautiful,' she murmured.

He downed his drink, and Kate saw he was ready to go. She picked up her cape and moved to the door. Silently they went down to his car—a silver-grey Mercedes coupé tonight, not the Rolls. Scott helped her in, but did not speak until they were quite a way from the flat.

In spite of the lateness of the hour, there was still plenty of traffic heading towards town. Scott drove fast but competently, and Kate, who did not normally like being driven, was not nervous with him, and was able to lean back in the comfortable black leather seat and relax.

'I know so little about you, other than the few details listed on your personnel card, and the fact that you're good at your job, of course,' he said, suddenly breaking the long silence, as they stopped at the Baker Street traffic lights.

'Unfortunately I haven't had the chance to look at your personnel card, Mr Jeffreys, so I know even less about you!'

He chuckled. 'I'm willing to answer any questions, if you are.'

'Fire away—but I'm afraid you're going to find my answers rather dull. My life's been pretty uncomplicated really. Happy schooldays and childhood, and no money problems—although my parents are far from rich,' Kate added, lest he get the wrong impression.

'They own a hotel, don't they?'

'A country hotel,' she corrected. 'Nothing on the scale of Blakes.'

'And all the nicer for it. They have none of the headaches either.'

'Not now, perhaps, but as with everyone else who starts a business, success didn't come easily, and they had to struggle for a number of years to establish themselves.'

'Aren't they disappointed you're not working with them?' he asked. 'I would have thought with your training, it was an ideal arrangement—then you could eventually take over.'

'Like most children—particularly only ones—I wanted to prove my independence—and sensibly they understood and haven't tried to make me feel guilty about it,' Kate explained.

He glanced at her. 'Obviously you're very close to them.'

'Very.'

'Do you intend going into their business eventually—or haven't you thought that far ahead?'

'That rather depends on who I marry.'

There was no time for further questioning, for they had arrived in Upper Brook Street. Scott drew to a halt outside an imposing grey block, and led her into the bar.

'Have you been here before?' Scott asked, over drinks— Kate having relented, and ordered a glass of white wine.

'I've been to Le Gavroche, but not since they moved from Lower Sloane Street.'

'It's a wonder to me how they ever managed to cook *anything* in the matchbox-sized kitchen they had there,' Scott Jeffreys remarked, 'let alone the gastronomic delights that earned them three Michelin stars.'

'Have you any ambitions along those lines for the French Room?' Kate asked. 'I gather you're spending quite a bit refurbishing it.'

'I think we'll have to be satisfied with a recommendation in Egon Ronay. To get even one Michelin star one needs an exceptional cook, and those are very few and far between.'

'If you give Tony Linden, the under-chef, a chance to show his real colours, I think you might be very pleasantly surprised. Raoul was one of Mr Blake's pets,' she said, referring to the French Room's head chef, 'and could do no wrong. Not that he's a bad cook, of course, just not a particularly creative one.'

Scott Jeffreys looked thoughtful. 'I'll go down to the kitchen and have a talk with him—on Raoul's day off, of course. I don't want to ruffle his feathers unnecessarily.'

'Don't be put off by Tony's age, and the fact that he's English,' Kate added.

'Only the French have the preconceived notion that only they know how to cook,' Scott smiled, 'and I'm always happy to give youth a chance.'

The manager, whom Scott had greeted by his first name, came over to tell them that their table was ready, and he led them downstairs to the restaurant.

Decorated in sage-green and bamboo, careful attention had been given to comfort, in the form of deep, padded velvet banquettes and chairs.

'I liked this room so much when I first saw it, I've asked David Mlnaric to re-design the French Room for us,' Scott Jeffreys told her, as he sat beside her on the banquette, so close that she could feel the pressure of his leg.

Kate wondered if he were going to spend the evening flirting with her, or if part of his intention *was* to discuss business. Somehow she was beginning to doubt the latter, and wondered if she had ever really believed it. No, she had been happy to accept it as an excuse to capitulate with some honour.

Choosing from the menu was made easier by the advice of the owner, and from the chit-chat that ensued beforehand, it was obvious he and Scott Jeffreys knew each other well.

'I hope you've brought us a young lady with a good appetite, for a change, Scott,' he said finally. 'Sometimes I feel guilty charging you for two meals, when one of them is sent back barely touched!'

'There's only one way to find *that* out, Albert,' Scott Jeffreys smiled. 'Bring on the food!'

Irrationally, the thought of all the other girls who had accompanied him before diminished some of Kate's pleasure in being here, but she was careful not to let it show, and commented with enthusiasm on the Chagall prints, and other modern paintings, that had been transferred from the original restaurant in Sloane Street.

'Are you keen on modern art?' Scott Jeffreys asked. 'From your disparaging comments on the refurbishing of my penthouse, I would have thought you were more of a traditionalist.'

'I'm one of those awful "I know what I like" kind of people. It covers a wide range of art, and also a good deal of ignorance!'

He chuckled. 'At least you're honest enough to admit it. I hate pretensions. Probably because of my background,' he mused. 'Although I managed to go to college, my appreciation of the good things in life had to be learned the hard way.'

He did not elaborate on his background further, and during the first part of the meal they talked of inconsequential things. But although inconsequential, they gave her a further insight into the man and his preferences. She was not surprised to learn that he was a keen sportsman, for he had an athletic build, and walked easily, his movements a compound of power and grace. He favoured the more vigorous activities; tennis, swimming and skiing, both on water and snow.

'I got into college on an athletic scholarship,' he confided, glancing up from the dessert menu. 'Harvard,' he added with a tiny smile. 'It was the only way I could have sneaked in, with my grades.'

Kate showed her surprise. 'Considering your business success, I find that hard to believe.'

'It's true, I assure you. The part of New York I hailed

from, you were a hero if you were good at sports and teased and bullied unmercifully if you paid too much attention to lessons—unless the teacher was young and pretty, of course!' He chuckled. 'My intention was to become a tennis pro—until I developed back trouble at the end of my first year in college. Then it was either improve my grades, or be thrown out. Not wanting to let down my parents or my high school—I was the first kid from there who'd ever made it to Harvard—I buckled down. Not having used my brain properly for the first nineteen years of my life, believe me, I found studying didn't come easy!'

'What made you decide to go into the hotel business?' Kate asked curiously.

'I just followed in my father's footsteps. He was a waiter for twenty-five years at the Thornton.' He named a famous New York hotel, now demolished. 'I used to work there in my holidays, and when I graduated, they offered me a job.'

'What made you move to Florida?'

'My father died, and I didn't want to continually be reminded of him at work, as well as at home. He never made much money, but in ways that *really* counted, he was quite a guy.' His voice was heavy with pride and affection.

'And what about your mother?'

A tender look came into his face. 'She's a lively sixty, with a passion for gin rummy.'

'Does she still live in New York?'

'No—in an apartment in Bal Harbour, Miami,' he said, then added. 'When she's not globe-trotting, that is. Right now she's in Sydney, Australia.'

'Staying at a Midas hotel, I hope?' Kate smiled.

'In the Presidential Suite, no less!'

The waiter appeared to take their order, and on Scott

Jeffreys' recommendation Kate settled on l'assiette du chef, which turned out to be a glorious collection of little desserts: a marquise chocolat, raspberry sablé, and a warm macaroon, together with spoonfuls of fruit sorbet and ice cream.

'Albert won't be disappointed this time,' Scott said with a smile, as he watched her tuck in. 'For a little girl, you have a man-sized appetite!'

'That's why I offered to go Dutch the first time we met, Mr Jeffreys! I was worried you might not be able to afford to feed me properly!'

He gave a broad grin. 'I don't know that I can! Having seen what you consume, I might take you up on that offer next time!' He slid closer along the seat, and because she was against a side wall she could not back away from him. His leg pressed hard upon hers and the pressure of his thigh was heavy. 'The name is Scott,' he said softly. 'I think we're friendly enough now to relax the formalities.'

'I won't call you Scott at work, though,' she warned.

'You really are old-fashioned, aren't you?'

'It's a sign of respect,' she argued.

'Using my surname doesn't indicate respect,' he disagreed. 'It just makes me feel old!'

Kate would like to have asked his age, but thought better of it. Some men were as sensitive about disclosing it as women.

'I'm thirty-five,' he said, reading her thoughts. 'You have a very expressive face, Kate, and it's easy to guess what you're thinking.'

'In that case I must remember to turn my face away whenever I have any unpleasant thoughts about you!'

Coffee appeared, and he was silent while their cups were filled.

'How about some brandy or a liqueur?' he suggested. 'You've relented enough to get through a half bottle of hock, so perhaps you'll relent some more.'

'I hadn't realised I'd drunk so much—no wonder I feel lightheaded.'

'I was hoping that had more to do with me than the wine!' Scott Jeffreys smiled.

'Do you usually have a potent effect on women?' she queried.

'I've been known to go to a few heads!'

'I shall have to take you in small doses then, Mr Jef—Scott,' Kate corrected swiftly. 'It would be fatal to become addicted.'

'You could do a lot worse,' he said, his ridiculously long lashes masking his eyes.

'And ,you could do a lot *better*,' she smiled. 'You're wasting your time on me. I'm an old-fashioned girl, with old-fashioned ideas.'

'Good,' he replied imperturbably. 'I hate girls who say "yes" too quickly. It takes all the fun out of the chase.'

'There are some girls who really don't want to be caught.'

'Is that a warning or a challenge?'

'I have a feeling you'd regard them as one and the same thing!'

He chuckled, but did not deny it. 'Putting you to the test might prove enjoyable.'

'You wouldn't be the first to try,' she warned. 'And so far I haven't succumbed.'

'Perhaps you've not been chased by an expert.'

'That's a familiar cry, if ever I heard one,' she mocked. 'Every man think he'll succeed where others have failed!'

'The difference is I *know* I will!'

'You don't suffer from an inferiority complex, do you?'

'I know that women find me attractive,' he said calmly, 'so where's the point in false modesty?'

'It could be interpreted as conceit,' she argued.

'Knowing one's worth is not conceit—but over-valuing it certainly is.'

'It's a very fine line—but I'll concede the point,' she smiled.

'You have the knack of making agreement sound like disagreement,' he smiled back, and motioned the waiter for the bill. 'But I enjoy arguing with you more than *speaking* to most other women!'

Kate found it difficult to remain untouched by such an unusual compliment, and could not prevent herself blushing. The change of colour did not go unnoticed and Scott's look was teasing. It made his square face appear remarkably handsome, and she felt the pull of his personality.

'It's a pity to end the evening so early,' he continued, 'Why don't we go on to Maybelle's and dance?' He named an exclusive nightclub in Mayfair.

'Isn't it a rather noisy place to discuss business?' she asked with deliberate naïvety. '*That* was the purpose of this evening, wasn't it?'

'Of course not,' he admitted disarmingly, and gave a slight smile, which lightened the depths of his dark eyes. 'And if you were to be equally honest, you'd admit you knew it.'

Kate shrugged resignedly, realising there was little point in denying it.

'I knew that until I went out with you, you wouldn't give me any peace.'

'Are you suggesting that once I had, I wouldn't want to repeat the experience?' he asked blandly, but there was a mischievous quirk to his lips. 'I've enjoyed myself immensely. Haven't you?'

'The meal was superb,' she prevaricated.

'How about the company?' he persisted.

'You do love to squeeze compliments out of people, don't you?' she said irritably.

'I love squeezing them out of *you*,' he corrected. 'You're so obviously determined to be on your guard with me.'

'I find it difficult to forget who you are,' she explained.

'Don't say you're in awe of me, because I won't believe you. There have been times when I've felt you dislike me, but from the way you answer back, I doubt if you've ever been scared of me.'

'You're right about that,' she admitted. 'I was brought up to believe that all people are equal, no matter who they are. Some pretty well-known guests have stayed at my parents' hotel over the years, and they made a point of ensuring that I met and talked to them all, from the time I was a small child.'

'Sounds a sensible way of being brought up,' he commented. 'I'd like to meet them some time.'

'Next time they come up to town, I'll introduce you,' she promised.

'Why don't you take me down to meet them instead?' he asked. 'I'd like to see where you come from.'

His request surprised her. 'Do you normally like to see where your employees come from?'

'Certain ones I do,' he replied easily. 'The ones I like to regard as my friends.'

'Girl friends, you mean?'

He laughed. 'You have a very one-dimensional view of me!'

'But you haven't denied my accusation?'

'Would you believe me if I did?'

CHAPTER SIX

THE interior of Maybelle's was intimately lit, and there was an excellent band playing melodic music of a bearable decibel level. It was also comparatively smoke-free, owing to the efficiency of the air-conditioning system. They were immediately shown to a table next to the dance-floor, and were greeted almost at once by the owner, Lord Mountford. At six feet six inches he was reputed to be the tallest peer in England. But his fame derived not from his height, but from the manner in which he had retrieved his family's declining fortune. Maybelle's—named after his wife, who heralded from America's Deep South—was the most exclusive and expensive nightclub in London, and although it had been open for a number of years, was still as popular as ever, and packed to the roof night after night.

He appeared to know Scott well, and asked how long he was staying in London, and if he had time to spend a weekend with his wife and himself at their home in the country.

'Bring whoever you like with you.' Heavily bagged eyes focused on Kate. 'I haven't seen you with Scott before, have I? What's your name, and who are you?'

Startled by the bluntness of his question, Kate looked at Scott, who laughed up at the man. 'Her name is Kate Ashton, and she works for me.'

'Brains too, eh?' Again his eyes rested on Kate. 'I know Scott wouldn't have anyone working for him who was *just* beautiful!'

Scott chuckled. 'Flattery will get you *nowhere* with this gal, Gerry. She's the original immovable object!'

'Then what's the problem? I've always taken it for granted you were the original irresistible force!' He smiled down at Kate. 'If Scott decides to give up on you, perhaps you'll allow me the chance?'

'Go ply your charms elsewhere.' Scott gave him a friendly punch on the arm. '*I* never give up!'

'Have you known him long?' Kate asked, as he moved off to the table behind them.

'Several years. He did a TV commercial for us, and we hit it off straight away.'

'A TV commercial?' she queried. 'I assume that was before he opened the club?'

Scott nodded. 'He was desperate to earn a few shekels—the family home was mortgaged to the hilt, and he was having difficulty meeting the payments.'

'How did he ever find the money to open Maybelle's?'

'It wasn't all that difficult. He had the right connections, and some of his friends had the money.'

'Were you one of them?' Kate asked curiously.

'Yes,' he replied, looking embarrassed. 'But I sold my share back to him some time ago.' He pushed back his chair, and turned his eyes to the floor. 'Shall we?'

Kate smiled, and stood up. For a brief instant Scott stayed next to her without touching her. There was so much intimacy in his glance that she trembled, then his arms drew her close and her trembling ceased as she fitted her steps to his. He was an excellent dancer, light on his feet, yet giving a suggestion of power; guiding her firmly, yet keeping his hold gentle. So he would be as a lover, she thought involuntarily, and with an effort, stifled an urge to nuzzle her face against his.

'Still can't forget who I am?' he teased. 'You've suddenly gone all tense on me.'

With an effort she went totally limp, and he gave a mutter of satisfaction, pulling her against him, moulding her body to his.

'Better,' he murmured. 'Much better.'

But it wasn't. It was much worse. His nearness was doing crazy things to her equilibrium; filling her mind with crazy thoughts. How easy it would be to lose complete control; to forget the dislike she had felt for him only a few hours ago, and remember only that she wanted him; had wanted him, in fact, from their first meeting. The acknowledgement frightened her, and aware of its danger, she tried to think of Mike. But though his image was clear no emotion of any kind accompanied it, and she felt almost as if she were looking at a likeness of someone she did not know. She moved her head slightly and her eyes met warm brown ones, their lids half lowered, but not enough to hide the slumbrous gaze. Her body grew warm and she was conscious of the pressure of his arms and the hardness of his chest against her breasts. His suit was fine wool, but it did not obliterate the steady beat of his heart, nor the steel-like quality of his muscles on his thighs pressed against hers, leading her into the swaying movements that passed for dancing on a crowded floor. The band broke into 'A New-Fangled Tango,' and without thinking, the words of the Lena Horne song ran through her mind. Yes, this *was* like making love standing up, and only the knowledge that he would guess the reason for her discomfiture, and laugh at her for it, made her resist the urge to pull back from him. Yet it was not the first time she had danced like this with a man—only the first time she had been sufficiently aware of one to be conscious of its significance.

His lips moved across her cheek, and she wondered how much further he was going to try and go before the evening was over. She remembered Hal Draycott telling her that his Friday night date always made herself available for the weekend, just in case he decided to spend the whole of it with her. How easy it would be to say yes to him, and how difficult to forget the encounter afterwards. It was this knowledge that she must keep in mind; unless she did, she would not have the strength to refuse him.

The thought was frightening. Never before had she had to bolster her resistance against a man. She had had many boy-friends, been strongly attracted to a few, but never sufficiently to make her fear her desires.

Scott's fingers caressed her skin, moving up and down her spine. With difficulty she focused her mind on the couples around them, staring at the women's clothes, and hoping her interest in fashion was strong enough to take her mind off Scott. But slowly, insidiously, her senses took over and, as their bodies swayed in unison, she became totally aware of every part of him; his firm bones and taut muscles; the tangy smell of his after-shave, his smooth skin, the warmth of his breath against her hair.

'Scott, you naughty boy! Why didn't you phone me today?'

The instantly recognisable throaty drawl of Dina Dalton made him pull sharply away from Kate, giving her a view of the slender blonde, who immediately drew back from her own partner, and edging Kate aside, flung herself into his arms.

'Because last night you told me you never wanted to see or hear from me again,' he answered.

'Only because you were so nasty about movie people, and refused to come out with us tonight.' The girl's eyes slid over Kate, and she gave a barely perceptive smile of acknowledgement before turning her attention back to Scott. 'But I didn't expect you to take me *this* seriously.'

'I take *all* your orders seriously, sweetheart,' Scott's voice was light but even as he spoke he looked at Kate. 'Perhaps you wouldn't mind if we changed partners, just while I try to reassure Dina I still love her.'

Kate minded very much indeed, but did her best not to show it.

'You're the boss!' she smiled, and as he took the girl into his arms, Dina's escort gently drew her into his own.

'We haven't been introduced, but I'm quite happy if you are?' he said with a distinctive American accent. 'This is one occasion when exchange is no robbery!'

But Kate was in no mood to respond to flattery. 'My name's Kate Ashton—I work for both Mr Jeffreys and Miss Dalton. Public relations,' she explained coolly and concisely.

'Gary Winston—I'm directing Dina's movie.'

He needed no further introduction, for though he was barely thirty, each one of his half dozen films had been blockbusters. Of medium height and slim build, he had an unruly mop of dark curly hair—permed, Kate suspected—and was dressed in a white suit and open-necked shirt, that would not have looked out of place on a pop star.

'Scott doesn't mind investing in movies, but he likes to keep himself aloof from them, and all concerned,' Gary Winston said, without rancour. 'Personally I'm inclined to agree with him. It's one of the reasons I refuse to live in Los Angeles, and have made my home in New York.'

As one number merged into another, he kept up a continual patter, seeming not to notice Kate's monosyllabic replies. At no point did Scott look as if he was preparing to return to her, and gradually Kate began to feel restive. Surely duty ended after a couple of dances, and no girl-friend, whatever her importance, merited leaving your current companion to the indefinite attentions of another man. Her eyes searched around the dimly lit floor for him, seeing him in the far corner. Blonde hair glowed against a dark shoulder as Scott's cheek lowered to rest upon a creamy one.

Anger welled up so strongly in Kate that, uncaring of the rudeness at her lack of explanation to her partner, she murmured 'Excuse me', and rushed from the floor. She was not going to stay here and watch Scott dance with Dina indefinitely. If he was so worried about offending her, then let him spend the rest of the night with her and her friends!

The doorman found her a taxi, and within fifteen minutes of leaving Maybelle's, she was back in her flat. Fortunately, Lucy was not yet home, so at least she would not have to face a barrage of questions.

She flung her cape and bag on her bed, and stood in the centre of the room. Disgust had replaced all other emotions, and she was quivering and alert. How dared Scott Jeffreys have treated her in such a humiliating manner? Was it because she worked for him that he imagined she could be discarded without thought for her feelings? Did he imagine she was so flattered to be in his company that she was willing to play dumb, until he was ready to honour her with his presence again? Well, by now he would have discovered otherwise!

Still, she had only herself to blame for what had happened tonight. She was well aware of his relationship with the actress, yet had accepted his invitation in spite of it, when for weeks she had stood resolute. But then, in her defence, he had told her it was to be a business dinner, and his invitation had been more of an order than a request. This had made it difficult for her to refuse him.

But no, who was she kidding?

It was not the thought of furthering her career that had made her go out with him, nor made her put on her most glamorous outfit. It had been a strong desire to attract him; a hope that their evening together would be the start of something more meaningful.

Frowning, Kate kicked off her shoes, something she always did when she was perturbed, and padded into the living-room. She would tidy up, and wash and put away the glasses. It would keep her thoughts—for a short while at least—off Scott Jeffreys. She plumped up the cushions on the couch and armchairs, and placed the nuts and crisps on a tray. But when she picked up the whisky tumbler he had used, the empty glass brought him so vividly to mind, it was almost as if he were still seated with it in his hands; his thick brown hair a silky cap around his well-shaped head; expressive eyes—that mostly mirrored irritation or amusement when he looked at her—now staring back at her with something else in their depths; something she had noticed the first time tonight, and had been unable to define.

She shook her head to clear it, and carried the tray into the kitchen; placing the nuts and crisps in their respective containers, before turning her attention to the glasses, and the plate and saucepan from a snack Lucy had prepared for herself.

She had just finished drying, when she heard a car door slam, then footsteps running up the stairs. It was probably Lucy, as the other tenants in the house were much older, and rarely came in after midnight. She waited expectantly to hear the key in the lock, but then the doorbell pealed, making her jump. There was only one person who would call at this time of night—Scott. He had come after her to apologise!

She debated whether to let him in or ignore him. He knew she was not in bed, because it was possible to see the flat lights from the street below, so pretending she was asleep and had not heard him was out of the question. In any case, it would be stupid. He had obviously realised he had behaved abominably, and wished to make amends. So why not allow him the opportunity?

Framing her lips into a cool smile—she had no intention of making things easy for him—Kate moved slowly towards the front door. As she did so, the bell rang again; a prolonged sound that conveyed his anxiety, followed by knuckles rapping a loud tattoo.

'Kate, open the door! I've forgotten my key.'

There was no way she could mask her disappointment. It was only Lucy, after all.

'Thank goodness you were back before me!' her friend said, as she came inside. 'Or is it? You look as if you've lost a fiver and found fivepence.'

'Lost an escort, is more like it,' Kate tried to make a joke of it. 'I was dumped in the arms of another man, while Scott proceeded to dance the night away with Dina Dalton.' Swiftly she recounted the whole story.

'I admire your courage,' Lucy said when she had finished. 'I don't think I'd have had the nerve to do it.'

'I was so furious, I just didn't think. But I'm sorry I was so rude to Gary Winston. It wasn't his fault, after all. I'll find out where he's staying, and phone and apologise.'

Sleep did not come easily or soundly to Kate, and she rose early, heavy-eyed and listless. A near-cold shower blew away some of her stupor, and after a hurried coffee, she set off on the drive to the Cotswolds.

A pampered weekend was just what she needed, and as

usual, her parents were only too happy to provide it.

Seated with her legs tucked beneath her, on the rug in front of the fire in their private sitting-room, she contentedly sipped a pre-lunch Martini, while her mother set the table in the adjoining dining-room.

'It's nice having you home, poppet,' her father lounging next to her in his favourite chintz wing chair, commented. 'When are you going to decide that the good life is down here and not in London?'

'Not for a long time,' she answered promptly, knowing he was only teasing her. 'I love coming to see you, but I'm not ready to allow you to retire just yet!'

He chuckled, and ruffled her hair. 'How are things going at Blakes?'

'Even more hectic than before the take-over.'

'Do you have as much to do with Mr Jeffreys as you did Mr Blake, or is he more of a figurehead?'

'I see a good deal of him,' she responded carefully, 'although my work-pattern's changed somewhat. And he's certainly no figurehead. He makes sure he knows what's going on everywhere.'

'I don't suppose that will last. Once the hotel's properly on its feet, he'll move to pastures new,' her father said. 'That's the way these tycoons operate. They get bored without a challenge.'

In pleasure, as well as business, Kate thought to herself, remembering how Scott Jeffreys had told her the reason he hadn't married was because no woman could hold his interest for long.

'He's offered me promotion,' she said aloud. 'He hasn't told me exactly what kind or what it will involve, but I'm pretty sure I'll have to move to one of his other hotels if I accept.'

'As Blakes is his only one in England, that will mean

another country,' her mother interjected from the dining-room. 'It sounds an exciting prospect, Kate darling.'

'I suppose so.'

'I'd be more excited by the prospect of a son-in-law,' her father grunted, coming into the conversation again.

Immediately Mike sprang to mind. It was a pity she had decided to stop seeing him. He was presentable, intelligent, and in view of his profession, would have made an ideal son-in-law. But she knew her parents would not approve of a marriage for any reason other than love, and that was the one emotion Mike had been unable to arouse in her.

'You don't sound very enthusiastic,' her mother spoke again, ignoring her husband's comment. 'Still not keen to work for a conglomerate—or just this particular one?'

Over lunch, Kate recounted the whole saga of Scott Jeffreys, from her first meeting with him to the previous evening, and only stopped when she saw her parents smile at each other.

'What's amusing you?' she demanded, surprised at their reaction.

'Your leaving the poor man in the lurch twice. Admittedly his behaviour last night wasn't exactly gentlemanly, but you should have waited and given him the chance to apologise. He must have liked you a lot to have forgiven you for the way you treated him the first time.' Mr Ashton smiled, to lighten his criticism. 'Let's be honest about it, darling, your behaviour on *that* occasion wasn't exactly ladylike, was it?'

'He shouldn't have tried to fool me,' Kate answered defensively.

'It was just a bit of fun,' her father said. 'What's happened to your sense of humour?'

'What was the reason last night?' she sneered. 'His idea of another bit of fun?'

'Business,' her father said promptly, before her mother could intercede. 'He obviously isn't in love with the Dalton girl, or he wouldn't have asked *you* out.'

'Lucky him, to be involved in business that also manages to give him so much pleasure!' Kate said derisively, irritated that her father could be so naïve as to judge all other men by his own code of conduct.

'If you dislike Mr Jeffreys so much, I don't understand why you want to continue working for him,' her mother came back into the conversation. 'Perhaps it would be better if you left.'

'I might just do that,' Kate said airily. 'Wendy Haynes,' she named a friend, 'has asked me to go into business with her. She does PR work for Granada Television, and has enough contacts to get us started.'

'It's a wonder you want to stay in PR,' her mother commented. 'If you have to earn your money promoting people like Dina Dalton . . .'

Kate had no intention of telling her parents it was not promoting Dina Dalton that was getting her down, but the actress's relationship with Scott Jeffreys. To admit to jealousy—and there was no other word for it—was tantamount to admitting . . . But that was ridiculous. Resolutely she concentrated on her crème brûlée, and banished all thoughts of Scott Jeffreys from her mind.

'Fortunately, not everyone's as difficult as Miss Dalton,' Kate said instead. 'And if I were my own boss, I'd be free to refuse a client if I didn't like them.'

During coffee, they discussed the merits of the idea, though neither her mother or father were willing to commit themselves. As usual, they preferred to allow her to make the final decision herself.

'Why don't you take the dogs out?' her mother suggested, when the maid came in to clear away the dishes. 'Your father's promised to make up a fourth for bridge with some guests, and I want to discuss tomorrow's menus with Maurice.' She referred to the chef, who had been with them since they had opened the hotel.

'Good idea,' Kate agreed at once. 'I don't get enough exercise in London, even though I live so near the Heath.'

An hour and a half later, invigorated after a walk in the woods bordering the hotel's grounds, Kate returned with the family's two golden retrievers.

'There's someone waiting to see you,' her mother told her, as she stepped into the hall with the panting dogs who, running back and forth chasing each other, had covered at least three times the distance she had. 'It's Mr Jeffreys,' Mrs Ashton went on. 'He's been here about an hour.'

'How on earth did he know where to find me?'

'Lucy told him. He called at the flat first.'

'You should have told him I was out visiting friends, and wouldn't be back till—'

'Why should I lie to the man?' her mother interrupted. 'If he could take the trouble to come down here to see you, the least you can do is hear him out.'

Kate realised her mother was right. She was behaving childishly and foolishly. By making excuses she was encouraging Scott to keep chasing her. She must face him and make it clear that she had no further interest in him.

'I'd better go upstairs and tidy myself first. It was terribly windy, and I feel as if I've been dragged through a hedge backwards!'

'You don't *look* as if you have,' her mother smiled reassuringly. 'And he has been waiting *most* patiently.'

For a moment Kate hesitated, then with a smile of

agreement, she turned the handle of the sitting-room door.

Scott Jeffreys was seated in her father's favourite armchair by the fire, and she was surprised to note how much at home he seemed to be. Somehow she had imagined his restless American dynamism would look out of place in this very English setting of oak and chintz.

Perhaps it had something to do with his mode of dress, she thought, as he stood up to greet her, for once again she was struck by the conservative cut of his clothes. They would not have looked out of place on a prosperous country squire, for though his tweeds were impeccably cut, they had a shabby quality that came from usage. He had either been back to his apartment to change, or kept a wardrobe at Dina Dalton's to save the bother. Certainly, he had had a tiring night; faint lines that had not been there the last time she had seen him marked his forehead and the corners of his eyes.

'Sorry to have kept you waiting,' she said, managing to sound not the least apologetic.

'Your mother was a most agreeable substitute—agreeable in both senses of the word,' he added pointedly.

'Unlike me, you mean?'

He was silent for a long moment. 'You certainly have a way of rubbing me up the wrong way,' he said finally.

'Me rub *you* up the wrong way?' Her tone was incredulous. 'Perhaps you've come here so that *I* can apologise to *you*!'

His wide mouth seemed to draw in. 'It wouldn't be a bad idea, at that.'

'Of all the—' Kate's voice shook with anger, and she half-turned her back on him. 'Go to hell!'

Fingers gripped her shoulders and spun her round to face him. 'I suppose you were expecting me to grovel?'

'Something like that,' she answered coolly. 'Your behaviour certainly warrants it.'

'I expected you to be more understanding. You know why I have to keep Dina sweet.'

His voice was harsh and she knew he was controlling his temper. But it blazed freely from his eyes and from the painful grip he still had upon her shoulderblades.

'She's no nickle-and-dime investment,' he told her. 'If she delays the movie with a tantrum it could be very costly.'

'So to keep her happy, you're willing to prostitute yourself?'

'What's that supposed to mean?' he asked, giving her a shake.

'Don't tell me you didn't go home with her last night?'

'Why, you . . .' Words failed him and he pushed her violently away from him. 'You've got the mind of a sewer rat!'

'And you've got the morals of one!' she retorted. 'So stop pretending.'

'Why should I pretend with you?' he demanded. 'We mean nothing to each other.'

'That's right—we don't,' she cried. 'You've used me as a convenience—when your girl-friend's away, or when you've quarrelled with her.' Her voice was a thread of sound. 'Well, I don't like being used!'

'If that were true, I wouldn't be here now,' he grated.

'Well, as far as I'm concerned you needn't have bothered coming. Your affair with Dina is your affair, and I'm not interested in explanations or apologies.'

'Perhaps you'd prefer action to words?'

Before she knew what he was going to do, he pulled her sharply into his arms. One hand gripped her head and the other held her tight as his mouth came down savagely upon hers. There was no tenderness in his kiss, only a determination to take possession of her, by force if need be. And force he needed, for she pummelled at him with her fists, trying to turn her head from side to side in an effort to evade the lips that were pressing hard against hers, the hands that moved possessively up and down her body. The blood pounded in her head and her heartbeats were so loud that they drowned all other sound, even the hard rasp of his breath.

But Scott showed no sign of weakening his hold, and gradually, against her will, she found herself responding to him; her mouth growing warm and soft, her limbs too as they moulded against him, losing herself in a wave of passion and longing that was frightening in its intensity.

His mouth lifted away from hers and he moved back slightly to look enquiringly into her eyes. What he saw there seemed to satisfy him, for he drew her close and began to kiss her again. This time he did it with slow deliberation, kindling her emotions like the devil kindling fire. His lips, his hands, worked their separate magic upon her until she gave a convulsive shudder and wound her arms around his neck, signalling her complete submission. Again and again they kissed, his thighs pressing hard on hers, his hands warm on her waist, her spine, caressing her shoulders and then cupping her breasts. They swelled to his touch, making every part of her body ache with the need of him, and the thudding of his heart against her ribs told her that he wanted her with an equal intensity.

She had been kissed before with equal expertise and passion, but never had she responded with such abandon, nor had to fight to keep some kind of control. Why was it that with this man she ached to run her fingers through his hair, to caress the thick column of his neck that rose from the burly shoulders? Perhaps it was his very strength and size that made her all the more responsive to his trembling need of her.

The sound of voices in the hall finally brought her to her senses, and she stepped back so that he was forced to release her.

His lids were lowered over his eyes and his wide mouth was slightly parted, the lower lip twitching slightly. A flush heightened his wide cheekbones, and as she watched him he ran a hand through his hair, ruffling the lighter flecked curls in the front.

'I'm not going to apologise for *that*,' he said huskily.

'I wouldn't expect you to, as you haven't had the decency to apologise for any of your behaviour.' Her voice was shaky and she swallowed hard. 'I suppose you consider all women fair game.'

'Don't be cheap!'

Kate caught her breath. 'Isn't that what you'd expect from someone with the mind of a sewer rat?'

'I made that remark in anger.' His lids lifted, showing glittering dark eyes. 'It's a mood you constantly rouse in me.'

'Then why don't we solve it once and for all!' she said coolly.

'I'd be more than happy to agree to anything you suggest,' he said, and his tone told her that he had completely misunderstood her remark.

'Then I suggest three months' notice.' She tilted her head defiantly. 'I'd leave sooner, but in view of my affection for Blakes, I feel it my duty to train in someone else.'

For several seconds Scott stared at her, then he spoke, his voice quiet and contemptuous. 'I assure you, you have no need to leave on my account. I'm more than willing to keep our relationship on a strictly business footing from now on.'

'Don't flatter yourself that you're the sole reason for my departure. I've had an offer from someone else, and the working conditions are more to my liking.'

'May I enquire who this "someone" else is?'

'It's not a competitor, so you don't have to worry that I'll give away any of the secrets of your success!'

'If I hadn't been confident of your discretion, I wouldn't have kept you in a position of trust,' he said harshly. 'But if your mind's made up . . .'

'It is.'

He shrugged. 'Then there's nothing more to be said, except that I'll expect you to continue to give of your best regarding Dina.'

'If you thought I wouldn't, then you don't know anything about me' she retorted.

'On the contrary, I think I know everything about you,' he said coldly, 'and most of it, I don't like!'

She was aware of his stride across the carpet and the slam of the door, before she lowered her head into her shaking hands.

The arrival of her mother who, from her bedroom window, had seen Scott's car draw away, forced Kate to try and regain a semblance of composure, though it was impossible to hide the tear marks on her face; impossible also to repair her make-up, and with her mouth devoid of lipstick, but so red from Scott's kisses that she needed none, it was not difficult for her mother to put two and two together.

'So you quarrelled again with him?' she said. 'That's a pity. I was hoping you'd kiss and make up, and that he'd stay on for dinner. He seemed to me to be utterly charming.'

'Well, as you can see, we did kiss,' Kate said bitterly, 'but we certainly didn't make up. In fact, I've given in my notice.'

Mrs Ashton shook her head. 'It's unlike you to be so impulsive, Kate. Couldn't a decision have waited until Monday.'

'I didn't want to give myself time to change my mind.'

'Why? Because you like him too much, or because he likes you too little?'

How well her mother knew her! 'Both,' she said simply, and leaned over to kiss her.

Later that evening, undressing for bed, she wondered if she had overreacted. Why hadn't she accepted Scott's appearance at her home at face value? The fact that he had taken the trouble to come down here—a two-hour drive—was surely an apology in itself. He was an aggressive and domineering man, and not one who liked to admit he was in the wrong. Yet she had expected him to grovel, to accept total responsibility, when clearly she was partly to blame; had been to blame from the very beginning. Because she had learned of his relationship with Dina Dalton, and assumed she was only a makeshift girl-friend, she had wanted to hurt him. She had behaved churlishly and petulantly, mistaking it for smart sophistication. But if she had acted with her usual intelligence he might have seen her as a person in her own right, and not just another pretty girl playing hard to get. To the last her foolish tongue had spoilt things, and now, for the short while she had left at Blakes, they would be on an even more uneasy footing than before.

CHAPTER SEVEN

HER prediction turned out to be completely accurate. When she saw Scott for the first time the following Wednesday, during lunch with Mike in the main restaurant, he merely nodded curtly down at her, before chatting pleasantly—and perhaps pointedly—for several minutes with Mike. Even when he summoned her to his office to tell her that she would be spending three weeks in Dublin with Dina Dalton on location, he behaved like a stranger—which in fact he was. After all, their friendship had barely reached beyond the starting gate.

'When will I be going, Mr Jeffreys?' she asked.

He gave no sign that he had noticed her reversal to his surname. Perhaps he remembered that she had told him she would not address him by his first name at work, although she had really meant in front of other members of the staff, not when they were alone. But it did not matter now.

'The last week in May. I gather the weather's even more unpredictable than here, so Gary wants to wait as late as possible in the hope that the sun will shine.'

'There shouldn't be any problems with publicity. I've discovered Miss Dalton had Irish grandparents on her mother's side, and I'll make sure I play up her happiness at visiting the country of her beloved ancestors!'

'Beloved ancestors!' he expostulated. 'They both died before she was born!'

Kate was surprised he was so familiar with her family background, but then if he *was* going to marry her . . .

'Still,' he went on, breaking into her thoughts, 'it's a good angle. The Irish are rather like us Americans—suckers for sentiment!'

'I might have to go over for a couple of days beforehand,' said Kate. 'Will that be all right?'

'Do whatever you think necessary.' Scott picked up a gold pen, and ostentatiously looked down at the papers on his desk. She did not need to be told he wanted her to leave.

'I've put an advertisement in *The Times* for a replacement,' she said, as she stood up. 'I don't know if you would like to interview the applicants.'

'Put an advert in *The Times*?' he echoed. 'Surely you didn't mean what you said the other day?'

'I never say things I don't mean.'

'Then you must be a paragon among women. They all say things they don't mean, when they're upset or in a temper.'

'I'm neither upset or in a temper now, and I still intend to go,' Kate said firmly.

'Once the refurbishing and alterations are completed, and the hotel's back in the black, I shan't spend much time here.' He raised a hand to silence her as she started to protest. 'I know you said I wasn't the principle cause of your departure, but in all honesty, I don't believe that's true.'

Kate shrugged. 'It doesn't really matter what you believe—I'm leaving just the same. I'm going into partnership with a friend of mine, doing the same kind of thing,' she told him, feeling some explanation was called for at this time. 'I have a yen to be my own boss.'

'It strikes me you've always been that!' For the first time Scott smiled, though it was purely perfunctory, for there was little humour in it. 'Perhaps you'd consider taking Blakes on as a client!'

'As long as my partner is the one who has to deal with *you*, Mr Jeffreys, I'm perfectly agreeable.'

He did not trouble to reply, and only the lightening of his eyes betrayed his annoyance. She had noticed they changed colour with his mood, glinting gold when he was angry, looking soft brown when he was teasing, and a deeper brown when he was aroused. But such thoughts were dangerous, and she pushed them away.

'You haven't told me whether you want to interview the applicants,' she reiterated. 'After I've sorted out the most suitable ones of course.'

'I'll trust to your judgment,' he said coolly. 'I'm sure with your strong loyalty to the hotel, you'll be just as particular as me.'

Thinking over his remark on the way back to her office, she decided he had not meant to be complimentary. He would be spending less and less time at Blakes in the future, and whoever took over her job would have more to do with the man he appointed as his successor, than himself—therefore her replacement, as long as she was competent, mattered little to him.

With her three-week assignment in Dublin in mind, Kate decided it would provide a good opportunity to make a final break with Mike, and agreed to see him the following Saturday, although she had previously pleaded a prior engagement with an aged relative.

Over the meal, in a restaurant in Chelsea, she began by telling him she was leaving Blakes.

'I can't believe it,' he said, looking shaken. 'You're part of the fixtures and fittings.'

Kate smiled. 'Well, they're all changing too!'

He caught her hand in his big, warm one. 'You know

what I *really* mean, Kate. The place won't be the same without you.'

'I don't flatter myself I'm indispensable—in fact I've already seen a couple of girls far more competent than I.'

'But I bet nowhere near as pretty!' Mike smiled back.

She disengaged her hand gently. 'I've got their phone numbers, if you'd care to find out.'

'You know I'm not interested in other girls,' he said softly.

'But I'm interested in other men—one in particular,' she lied, knowing from past experience that he would be more inclined to accept her rejection as final, if he believed there was another man involved. 'I'm sorry, Mike, but I thought it best to tell you straight away.'

'Who—who is it?' he asked. 'Anyone I know?'

Wildly she sought for an answer, but none came to mind.

'I don't think so,' she said, still desperately thinking, as the piped music changed to the theme from a film she had recently seen—a film directed by Gary Winston. Of course!

'Gary Winston,' she said. 'I met him through Miss Dalton. He's directing her film.' Well, at least *that* part of her story was true, she consoled herself.

'I'm impressed,' he said. 'He's a very talented guy. Are congratulations in order, or are you just good friends?'

'Congratulations are a bit premature,' she smiled, and reached out to touch his arm. 'I hope we can go on being good friends, though.'

'Perhaps in the future. I'm too much in love to think of you in those terms just yet.' His head tilted and his hair gleamed blond in the light. At this moment he looked no older than herself, though she knew him to be eight years her senior. But fair men had a tendency to look young, and Mike would still look boyish when he was in his fifties.

'Let's enjoy our final evening together, anyway,' he said with a forced smile, and chose a neutral topic. 'Have you heard anything about the fraud investigation?'

'I mentioned it to Mr Jeffreys last week, but he seemed rather vague about it.'

'Obviously you haven't bothered to look through that file in your safe.'

'I haven't had time,' she confessed. 'Dina Dalton-watching is a full-time occupation!'

'Well, as long as the information is under lock and key, the people concerned aren't likely to suspect they're being watched, and try to make a run for it.'

Kate tapped her handbag. 'I carry my safe key around with me wherever I go. Mr Jeffreys' instructions,' she explained.

'You'd better make sure you don't get your handbag stolen,' he teased. 'If it should fall into the wrong hands . . .'

'It hasn't got "safe, top secret", marked on it,' she laughed. 'It's just an ordinary-looking gold Banham.'

For the remainder of the evening, they discussed her future prospects as a freelance PRO, and though he offered some helpful suggestions, she was glad when the evening ended.

The weeks until her departure passed swiftly. Although she was occupied in the main with the actress, she could not leave all her other duties to Janet, nor the interviewing of applicants for her own position, who were numerous. She finally chose a girl somewhat older than herself, who had worked for British Airways for several years.

It was difficult to avoid seeing Scott, particularly when he decided to accompany Dina to the television studios on several occasions. He was always friendly, but cool, adopting the perfect employer's manner, in fact, and taking her lead from him, Kate responded in kind.

In spite of her dislike of the actress, Kate had to admit she was more than just a beautiful face with a good script. She handled her television appearances with skill, and at the studios—where Gary had allowed Kate to see some of the rushes—was proving to be more than just a good comedienne, as her first film had shown, but a performer of some depth.

Gary had completely forgiven Kate for her rudeness to him on the first occasion they had met, and seeing her with Dina, had taken the opportunity to ask her out. Kate liked him sufficiently to agree, and he now occupied most of her free evenings.

As things turned out, she did not have to go to Dublin to set up any of the press or television interviews, but managed them all by telephone. As Scott had said, the Irish were a sentimental race, and the fact that Dina Dalton was of Irish descent was sufficient to ensure a good response.

'You look as if you didn't sleep last night,' Janet commented a few days prior to Kate's departure.

'I didn't get to bed till four,' she confessed.

'Burning the candle at both ends won't help you forget.'

'I'm not trying to forget anyone or anything—just having a good time.' Kate looked through her diary to remind herself of her appointments for the following day. 'I'd like to do some shopping before I go,' she said. 'I need a new raincoat. That's a necessity, if all the jokes about the Irish weather are true!'

'The most important thing to take with you is your sense of humour.'

'That's the one thing I must leave behind,' Kate replied. 'Mr Jeffreys likes me to take Miss Dalton seriously.'

Raising her arms in mock horror, Janet retreated, and Kate forced herself to concentrate on answering a batch of complaints.

As Tuesday drew nearer, Kate grew more despondent. She was not looking forward to being on location with Dina, nor having to spend three weeks with Gary, who would expect her to be with him every evening. He was used to the free-and-easy atmosphere of the movie world and the situations and arguments he derived to entice her into bed with him—which at first she had found amusing—were beginning to pall.

She spent Saturday sorting through her clothes and, as always before she went on holiday—even working ones— came to the conclusion she had nothing to wear. A new raincoat would definitely not suffice!

A hurried trip to Knightsbridge on Monday afternoon—if, as Scott Jeffreys had suggested, she was her own boss, then why shouldn't she take the time off?—where she bought several new outfits, served to boost her morale, for though she could never compete with Dina in the beauty stakes, there was no shortage of men who found her attractive. Even Scott had wanted her. She shied away from the memory, like a frightened horse. He had only wanted her to fill in a few free hours when Dina had been away, or they had quarrelled. She wondered what he would do during the girl's absence, and for an instant regretted her own departure. It would have been interesting to know if he would have contacted her. It was a foolish notion to assume even for a second. At all their meetings, he had given every indication that he had not forgiven her for her behaviour, the day he had come down to see her at her parents' home.

On Tuesday morning a radio cab collected Kate and took her directly to the airport. Gary and the second camera unit, who were filming the Irish scenes, arrived at almost the same time, and they queued up together to have their luggage weighed. Extras were being recruited in Dublin, and supporting members of the cast would be arriving as needed.

The crew seemed to take it for granted she was with Gary, and she was sure he had warned them to keep away from her, so that he could occupy all her spare time. Well, she would allow him to do so for the moment, but she had no intention of fighting for her honour every single night of her stay!

With his arm around her waist, he shepherded her towards the departure gate, and only stopped when they heard a hubbub behind them.

'It's Dina,' Gary murmured, glancing round.

Kate followed suit, and saw the actress, muffled to the eyeballs in black diamond mink. But it was her escort who commanded her attention as he swung along with his characteristic ease, so confident of his power and position that he could afford to look relaxed. Obviously Scott had come to see her off. Kate was aware of him looking around and sensed he was searching for her. Forcing herself to remember she was here because of her job, she moved forward to greet Dina.

'There were only three photographers outside,' the girl complained immediately.

'One of them was an agency man, and he'll make sure all the papers are covered. You'll be meeting the full Irish press at Dublin airport.'

'Let's hope I'm feeling up to it. I hate a fuss *after* I've flown. If you hadn't a memory like a sieve, you'd have remembered that from the day you met me here—or rather *didn't*.'

Kate bit her lip. Perhaps she had been rather thoughtless, but there was no need for the girl to tell her off in front of Gary, and in such a loud voice that other passengers had turned round to look. It was obvious where Scott's sympathies lay, though, for he favoured her with a hard stare.

'I hope you've paid more attention to the rest of the arrangements,' he drawled. 'I suggest you check with Dina first, even if it means forgoing some of your time with Gary.'

Kate was so angry that she spoke without care. 'May I remind you that you and I are two of a kind, Mr Jeffreys. We both always put business before pleasure!'

The silence was electric, then Scott shrugged. 'Forgive me.' His tone mocked her. 'I had forgotten.'

'Now we're all friends again, let's go through, darling.' Dina was suddenly in a better mood. 'We've plenty of time to browse around the duty-free shop, and you can buy me some perfume.'

So Scott had decided to accompany Dina to Ireland. For how long? Kate wondered. In view of his busy work schedule, whatever the length of his stay it was unlikely to be solely for a holiday. Perhaps he had decided to investigate the possibilities of opening a hotel there. Although it was not one of the principal capitals, it was considered prestigious, particularly among Americans.

Some fifteen minutes later, queueing behind him to board the plane, she found her assumption to be correct.

'I've had it in mind for some time,' he said in answer to her enquiry, 'and it seemed a good idea to kill two birds with one stone.'

'I'm sure it will make Miss Dalton's visit more enjoyable,' she commented.

'But not yours—obviously!'

The air hostess requesting their boarding passes saved

her replying, and she and Gary were shown to seats behind Scott and Dina. Because of union rules, even the crew were travelling club class—there was no first on the short hop to Dublin. But there were free drinks, and it did not take long before most of them were in a merry mood. The noise of the engines prevented Kate from hearing Dina's conversation with Scott, but she could not avoid the intimate gestures the girl lavished on him, her hand resting frequently on his arm, ruffling his hair, or rubbing his leg.

'Boy, she can't keep her hands off him,' Gary sounded amused. 'I wish I could say the same for you!'

'That's because you're not my sugar-daddy!'

'Nor is Scott Dina's. Let's face it, sweetheart, he's good-looking and intelligent enough to be loved for himself alone.'

How right Gary was. Kate recognised, with her usual honesty, that her remark had been brought on by jealousy; a longing to be in Dina's place, beside Scott. She hated herself for the admission, and found herself wishing she could return on the next plane home. This did not bode well for a happy stay, and by the time they touched down at Dublin, after spending the remaining half hour trying unsuccessfully to devise a plausible excuse for leaving, her nerves were stretched to breaking point.

Fortunately the flight had been a good one for Dina. She posed happily for the photographers, and chatted eagerly to the reporters, giving them lots of amusing data about the character she was playing, and stressing her delight that at long last she was able to visit the country of her forefathers.

'I feel as if I've come home,' was one quote that found certain favour.

'Nobody's better than Dina at saying the right thing at the right time,' Scott said in an aside to Kate.

'Perhaps she doesn't really need me?'

'Perhaps she doesn't. But I do.' His voice was low.

'You never give up trying, do you?' she snapped, and turned her back on him. But he sidestepped in front of her and she found herself facing him again.

'Sometimes you behave more like an overgrown school-girl than an intelligent woman.' His voice was quiet, but she recognised the anger in it.

Kate longed to reply that with him she felt more like an overgrown schoolgirl than an intelligent woman; like one with a crush on her first boy. Instead, she had to keep up her brittle, couldn't-care-less act, so that he would never guess the effect he had upon her. An effect she was beginning to recognise for what it was.

Her heart began to pound so loudly that she felt as if she were going to faint, and her expression must have given her away, for he put his hand on her arm.

'What's wrong, Kate? Are you feeling ill?'

'Slightly faint,' she mumbled. 'It's warm in here.

Instantly he put his arm around her, half leading, half carrying her to a seat.

'Stay there,' he ordered. 'I won't be a minute.'

In fact he was several, as he went upstairs to the bar, returning with a glass of brandy. 'Drink this—it will help.'

She shook her head. 'I hate the taste of it.'

'Stop behaving like a spoilt child, and do as you're told,' he said, and held the glass to her lips, forcing her to drink it all, in spite of the face she made after the first sip. 'Now sit back with your eyes closed,' he advised. 'I'll come back for you when we're ready to leave.'

She was glad to obey and remained quietly seated, only vaguely aware of the people around her. The airport, though ultra-modern, was small and intimate and there was none of the hustle and bustle of the larger capital cities. A young Irish couple, waiting to meet relatives on the next flight due in, sat down beside her, and immediately struck up a conversation.

'Early summer's the best time to tour Ireland,' they assured her, in a soft brogue.

'I'm afraid I'm here to work,' she told them. 'But I'll certainly take some time off to go round Dublin.'

They spent some time advising her what to see, but stopped talking when they heard a commotion, and saw Dina sweep by, still surrounded by the press and a small crowd of hangers-on.

'Isn't that Dina Dalton?' the young man enquired.

Kate smiled, 'Yes, I believe it is.'

'I read she was coming over to make a film,' his wife said.

'I bet she's staying at the Berkeley Court.' Her husband guessed correctly, though Kate did not tell him so. 'We'll go in there for a drink with Sean and Eileen. Perhaps we'll catch another glimpse of her.'

Feeling somewhat better, Kate stood up, and with a murmured thanks for their helpful suggestions, made her way to the exit.

'I thought I told you to wait for me?' Scott was beside her and she saw that Dina was listening. The last thing she wanted was to excite the girl's jealousy. The next few weeks were going to be difficult enough without that. Instantly she turned to Gary who had been caught up in the interviews, and with a warm smile, took hold of his arm. She would have to use him as a means of disarming the actress's suspicions. It was surprising that Dina, for all her talent and beauty, should be jealous of her. Perhaps it had to do with some kind of insecurity in her background, or just plain possessiveness. It could even be a mixture of the two.

The crew set off for Dublin in a hired coach, large enough to take all their camera equipment and luggage—as well as some of Dina's, whose fifteen suitcases would not fit into the boot of her limousine. In the normal course of events, Kate would have travelled with them, but instead she accompanied Gary in a black Mercedes, following behind Scott and Dina in a matching white one.

The journey to Ballsbridge, where the hotel was situated, only took about thirty-five minutes, and would have been considerably less had there been a motorway. But with only two lane traffic for most of the way, the car was unable to pick up speed. The scenery was uninteresting; rows of houses and shops in the main, though the former were well kept, and the vast majority had neat blinds instead of net curtains at the windows.

Until they reached Trinity College, Kate was beginning to wonder what tourists found to rave over in Dublin. O'Connell Street, although an impressively wide thoroughfare, thronged with pedestrians, was dirty and litter-strewn, and other than Clery's, a large department store, the shops and buildings were quite characterless. Even the Post Office with its colonnaded front, did little to fire her imagination, though it was historically a meeting place in times of crisis—usually of the political kind, she surmised, in view of Ireland's troubled history. But the Georgian frontage of the college, with its splendid statues of Burke and Oliver Goldsmith in the cobbled front courtyard, and the Bank of Ireland that had once served as the House of Parliament, were most imposing, as were the tall Georgian houses—mainly offices now—with fanlights above brightly painted front doors, overlooking neatly kept squares.

The modern design of the Berkeley Court Hotel, set in a quiet side road in one of Dublin's most fashionable areas, left nothing to be desired either. A uniformed porter, dressed in brown and cream to match the awning covering the entrance, ushered them inside, while the manager welcomed Dina with a large bouquet of flowers.

'I'll take you up myself,' he said, and whisked his three-star guests away, while Kate waited with the crew, like ordinary mortals, to register, and be assigned their rooms.

Her own was on the fourth floor, and was compact, but luxurious, with wallpaper, bedspread and curtains in a matching Paisley design of warm reds and golds. There was a half-canopied queen-size bed, a telephone in the bedroom and bathroom, and a colour television set that showed in-house movies.

'We're showing "Catch as Catch Can", this week, in honour of Miss Dalton,' the bellboy named Dina's first film. 'Do you think you could ask her for an autographed photograph? The manager doesn't like us to bother the guests.'

'Of course,' Kate agreed, and asked his name, so that Dina could personalise it.

Kate had arranged to meet Gary downstairs for a drink at seven-thirty, and she was glad they would be dining at a communal table with the crew on their first night, for it meant she would not need to entertain him. Deciding to take a bath before changing, she lay in the warm water and tried not to think of Scott and Dina. But her thoughts could not be stifled, and all too easily she envisaged them together. Was his room on a different floor or did they have communicating suites? She did not know how Irish hoteliers regarded illicit liaisons and decided, in any event, that film stars and millionaires were a law unto themselves.

It was strange to think she and Scott would be sleeping under the same roof tonight, possibly only separated by a few yards. His suite might even be directly above hers. The sound of running water overhead set her pulses racing so fast that she could not help laughing at herself. For one foolish moment she had thought he might drop through the ceiling! With a sigh, she added some more hot water, then leaned back again and relaxed.

But not for long. A couple of minutes later the telephone near the bath rang.

'Are you decent?' Scott's voice questioned. 'If you are, how about joining me in my suite for a drink?'

'Where—where are you?' she asked, so flummoxed she was not certain what to answer.

'In the tub,' he said, deliberately misunderstanding her. 'Don't you wish you were with me?'

'No!'

He chuckled. 'I wish you were. I've got two in my bathroom, and the other one looks pretty lonely.'

'I'm sure you'll have no difficulty in filling it,' Kate said waspishly.

'Except I'm not interested in second-best. It's you I want.'

Anger swamped her. Did he think she could be taken in by his flattery? He only saw her as a pleasant hors d'oeuvre, before he concentrated his main endeavours on his favourite dish!

'Then I suggest you start running the cold water, otherwise you're in for a frustrating time!'

He chuckled again. 'If I promise to greet you fully clothed, will you have that drink with me?'

'As it happens I'm also in the bath,' she said unbendingly. 'And I'll be staying in it for the next quarter of an hour. Then I'm dressing, and going down to the bar to have a drink with Gary.'

'No problem. I'll join *you* then. I'm not shy about seeing you in the tub!'

For answer, Kate slammed down the receiver, gaining a childish satisfaction from the gesture. Without doubt, he was the most maddening man she had ever met!

Perhaps. But at times, the most lovable too. The admission startled her, though she was aware it had been forming in her subconscious for some time. But she had fought shy of it, refusing to allow it to surface, preferring to see the strength of her attraction to Scott as a purely physical emotion. She loved him; had loved him almost from the first. It accounted for her overreaction when she had learned that he planned to marry Dina, and the antagonism he continually aroused in her. It also explained why she had become increasingly restless about her relationship with Mike, and why she found it so difficult to interest herself in any other man. Even Gary, whose success and aura of glamour were sufficient to make him desirable in most women's eyes.

But the recognition of her love gave her no joy; how could it when she knew he did not love her, and perhaps was incapable of love in the way she herself defined it? Certainly he desired her—but then as a man in the prime of life, he probably desired most pretty girls—and had indicated his admiration for her intelligence and spirit. But it would be foolish, even dangerous, to imagine the reason for his continued interest in her, in spite of all she had said and done to discourage it, was because he genuinely cared for her. So where did that leave her? Back where she had started, for there was no way she could put him out of her life for another three weeks. She had a job to do, and her own pride would not allow her to act unprofessionally and leave it. On the other hand, she could not continually treat him as a leper; they would be thrown together a good deal socially, and it could prove an embarrassment for others.

No, difficult as it might be, she had to change her tactics towards him, and respond less aggressively, while at the same time ensure that she did not reveal her true feelings. If he ever guessed, he might become even more persistent, and caring for him as she did, she was not certain she would have the will-power to resist him—or even want to. After all, wouldn't a few weeks or months with Scott be better than no Scott at all? Yet even as the thought was forming, she was dismissing it. An affair would not satisfy her, but only make it harder to forget him when the time came.

It was a dispirited girl who made her way down to the oak-panelled bar at seven-thirty, though no one looking at her would have guessed. Dressed in one of her new outfits—a filmy silk chiffon print in soft greens, through which her arms and shoulders gleamed with the lustre of a pearl—she knew it was a terrific morale booster, as was the heavier than usual application of make-up. She had felt too drained to bother over-much with her hair, and it fell loosely around her shoulders, enhancing the faint air of vulnerability that clung to her, and came from the awareness of her feelings for Scott.

But she was determined to drown this awareness, even for a short while, and had several glasses of champagne before dinner.

'Hey, you'd better watch out,' said Gary. 'I don't want you passing out on me *before* we eat!'

'How about afterwards?' she smiled.

'It depends at what stage!' His expression made his

meaning obvious. 'Come on,' he caught hold of her hand and pulled her up, 'let's join the gang!'

Over the excellent dinner around a large table in the elegant cream and gold dining-room, the talk centred on the movie industry, with gossip about its personalities, and the inevitable discussion on the dire state of its finances, particularly in England. There seemed to be some resentment that once again American money was responsible for keeping them in work, and anger that British financiers were so reluctant to invest, even in a sure fire winner.

Kate could not help smiling to herself at the assertion. From what she had read, public taste was far too fickle for any film to be a 'sure thing'.

'Shall we have coffee and brandy outside?' Gary suggested quietly to Kate as the waiter appeared with the cups. 'I don't know about you, but I'd like to talk about something other than movies for the rest of the evening.'

Kate smiled her agreement and stood up. 'No brandy for me, though. Just coffee, please.'

But she had barely swallowed her first mouthful, when she heard her name being paged, and excusing herself, crossed the blue and gold carpeted lobby to answer it.

'There's a telephone call for you, Miss Ashton,' she was informed at reception. 'We've put it through to one of the booths.'

He indicated which one, and slightly puzzled—she was not expecting anyone to telephone—Kate picked up the receiver.

It was Dermott Sullivan, one of Ireland's most famous entertainers, who hosted a popular late-night chat show on one of the national channels. Kate had already had some communication with him in London, and he had shown a good deal of interest in having Dina as a guest on his show.

'I know it's a terribly short notice,' he apologised, 'but I have a free slot tomorrow. The author I intended interviewing is down with 'flu, and I've only just heard.'

'I don't know whether Miss Dalton is free,' Kate answered cautiously. Knowing the actress's temperament, she might interpret the request as being second-best choice. 'I'll have to speak to her, and find out. I'll ring you back probably within the hour.'

Returning to Gary, she explained what had happened. 'I'm going to be a while, so I think I'll say goodnight now. It's been a long day, and I think I'll turn in afterwards.'

The actress's suite was on the top floor—where else *would* she be? Kate thought cattily, and fleetingly wondered whether Bruce Raymond, Dina's co-star, who was arriving later that evening, was being given equal billing!

Scott answered her knock—not wanting to surprise them, in case they were in bed, she had rung to tell them she would be coming up, briefly explaining why—and he ushered her through the entrance lobby into a spacious lounge/dining-room. Traditionally and comfortably furnished, its predominant colours were cream and burnt orange, and the massed flower arrangements were in the same hues. The bed could be glimpsed through the archway connecting the two rooms, and she noted that the cover was still on, and undisturbed.

Dina, glamorously attired in gold satin lounging pyjamas, that clung to her body, revealing rather than concealing her full breasts, was seated on a couch by the window, and a full bottle of champagne stood in an ice-bucket on the low glass table in front of her.

'Care for some coffee?' asked Scott, indicating the pot on a trolley nearby.

Kate shook her head. She did not intend to linger, or socialise, but make the meeting as brief as possible. The sight of the two of them in such relaxed intimacy, was almost unbearable.

Scott indicated an armchair, and seated himself in the one opposite. He was casually dressed and had never looked younger nor more attractive, his body firm and strong in tight-fitting slacks and silk jersey sweater that bore the stamp of the finest Italian knitwear.

Kate immediately got down to business, and was surprised when Dina readily agreed to appear on the show.

'Scott thought it would be silly of me to refuse as I'm free.' She smiled mistily at him. 'And as he always knows what's best for me . . .'

'Would you like me to arrange for you to appear *with* Miss Dalton?' Kate asked, turning to look at him. 'After all, your visit here is partly business.'

'If I'd wanted any personal publicity, I'd have told you myself,' he said pleasantly.

'It's my job to check,' she said stiffly.

'I'm glad you listened to my advice—better late than never, I suppose,' the other girl said pointedly.

'It might be a good idea if Bruce were to appear with Dina, though,' Scott suggested. 'I'm sure *he'll* be agreeable.'

'Good idea,' Kate answered briefly. 'I've seen him interviewed on TV at home, and he comes over well.'

'I hope you're not suggesting that I don't,' the actress bridled.

'Kate's a great fan of yours,' Scott jumped to her defence. 'I'm tired of hearing her praise you.'

Surprised, Kate stared at him. His eyes, so clear a brown that they looked tawny, stared back at her, their expression unreadable.

'Really?'

'Yes, really,' Kate echoed as confirmation.

Dina's good humour was restored, and she smiled. 'I hope Gary won't be resentful at not being included. He's something of a star in his own right.'

'He hates being interviewed on chat shows,' said Kate. 'Highbrow magazines are more his forte.'

'I'd hardly call *Playboy* highbrow,' Dina commented. 'He was in *that* last month.'

'It has a serious side to it,' Scott smiled. 'But only a few intellectuals like myself buy it for that reason!'

'That's because the only girl *you* have eyes for is me,' Dina purred, and crossed over to perch on the arm of his chair.

Kate stood up abruptly. 'There's nothing further to discuss at the moment, and I promised Mr Sullivan I'd get back to him as soon as I could.'

She was at the lift door when Scott called her name, and she turned to look at him.

'How about acting like a real American tourist, and doing the sights with me tomorrow?'

'Have you asked Dina's permission?'

If she had thought to embarrass him, she was mistaken. 'Until I'm married, I'm free to see whom I choose, when I choose.'

'I'm delighted to hear you intend being faithful *afterwards*,' she said sarcastically, forgetting her vow to be polite.

'I have a great respect for middle-class morality. That's why when I do decide to marry, I want to make sure it's for ever.' He watched her silently for a moment, as if trying to fathom her thoughts. 'Well?' he said. 'How about it?'

Kate had little to do, and he probably knew it, therefore

she had no valid excuse for refusing—and hadn't she decided anyway to stop treating him like a leper?

'Okay,' she shrugged, and stepped into the lift. 'What time shall we meet?'

'Eight-thirty. We can have breakfast together first.'

Not giving her time to object, he turned away, and the lift doors closing immediately blotted him from sight.

CHAPTER EIGHT

WITH his usual punctiliousness, Scott arrived downstairs exactly to time. Bright of eye, and freshly shaved, he was dressed as casually as last night, but more warmly, in cashmere sweater and tweed trousers. Obviously paying court to two women at the same time did not affect him, and Kate wished she were equally adaptable.

In spite of a day that had been long and tiring—she had had to wait up to speak to Bruce Raymonde about his appearance on the chat show—her night's sleep had been fitful. Several times she had awoke to imagine herself in Scott's arms, and each time her longing to be with him, and the knowledge that he was in the arms of another woman, made it difficult to fall asleep again.

'Unpleasant dreams?' he greeted her cheerfully. 'You look as if you're ready to go to bed, not just getting up.'

'Thanks,' she said dryly. 'There's nothing like compliments to make a woman feel good!'

'Obviously you're a girl whose sense of humour deserts her in the morning!'

'As it happens I'm usually full of the joys of spring,' she asserted truthfully. 'I had too much to drink before and during dinner last night, and it's left me with a headache.'

'Have you taken anything for it?' He was immediately solicitous.

Kate shook her head. 'I hate taking pills.'

'And I hate people who hate taking pills!' he stated irritably. 'Two aspirins won't do you any harm, or would you prefer to suffer?'

'I guess you're right,' Kate sighed. 'I'll ask the waiter for some.'

'I've hired a car,' he told her over bacon and eggs, 'and made a few enquiries about what to see. It's such a lovely day, I thought we'd drive out of town, and admire the scenery.'

'I believe Gary's shooting his first scene this afternoon down by the canals. I had promised to go and watch.'

He put down his knife and fork. 'Are you serious about him, or is Mike still the one you care most for?'

Obviously he did not know she and Mike had split up, and she had no reason to illuminate him.

'Why do you ask?'

'Because I want to know.'

'I—I'm not sure,' she bluffed.

'Well, until you make up your mind, I have as good a call on your time as either of them—better, in fact. I'm paying your wages.'

'Not for much longer,' she reminded him.

'I hope by that time you'll like me enough to put me first.'

'I could say the same for you,' she answered more tartly than she had intended. 'But I won't.'

But Scott was in too good a humour to either notice or care. 'You just have!' he said, and was still chuckling when the waitress came over with the bill.

Before leaving, Kate wrote a note for Gary. She knew he would be far too wrapped up in his work to really care whether she turned up or not, and this assuaged her pangs of guilt to a degree.

With a scenic guide on her lap, they headed towards the mountains, and within an hour were driving through breathtaking countryside; deep valleys, gentle lakes and streams, and sweeping, rolling hills. Well worn nature trails through forests of fir trees and pine, as well as picnic sites, testified to the popularity of the route, but there was very little traffic. In fact they hardly passed a car, and the only hold-up was caused by a flock of sheep crossing the narrow, winding road.

Kate was particularly intrigued by the neatly stacked bricks of peat, left to dry in the wind and sun, before being collected for fuel by the owners of the land, divided into allotments bearing their names. It reminded her that although a modern country in most ways, Ireland had not been completely converted to the twentieth century.

'Like you, it has a charm of its own,' Scott commented gallantly, when Kate voiced her thoughts.

She smiled at the man at the wheel. He was holding it lightly, his long fingers curled over the rim, one elbow resting on the side of the door. The breeze from the open window was dishevelling the top of his hair and it gave him a devil-may-care look. As though sensing her scrutiny, he also smiled. Her heart thumped in her throat. Satan with a smile. The description came into her mind unsought, but it remained there. It was an apt description, for he had the charm of the devil; the luck too, for success had come easily to him. True, he worked hard to maintain it, but then lots of men worked equally hard and did not attain one iota of this man's achievement.

'Mmm!' Kate breathed in the freshly scented air appreciatively, as they reached Glenmacree, and parked the BMW, so they could get out and have a better view of the waterfall, glinting like silver in the sunlight as it cascaded down the rocks into the valley below. 'I wish I never had to go back to the city.'

'You don't have to,' Scott said immediately. 'I'll buy you a little rose-covered cottage, and we'll live happily ever after in it.'

Kate laughed. '*I* might, but I can't see you enjoying the solitude for long. You'd soon miss business.'

'I'd have you—what more could any man want?' he said huskily, and pulled her into his arms.

She had no chance to resist him; no chance to avoid his mouth which came down full on hers. It was warm and gentle, as were the hands that moved down her back to her waist, drawing her close against him. She felt the warmth radiating from his body, and breathed the tangy scent of after-shave lotion, and the more intimate scent of the man himself.

'It's like holding a bird,' he whispered against her lips.

'Give me the chance, and I'll fly away,' she whispered back.

'Not yet,' he said thickly, and went on kissing her, moving his lips along the fullness of her cheek to the lobe of her ear, and then along the curve of her neck. She felt his hand on the zip of her jacket, but he made no effort to undo it or even to hold her in a more intimate way, which surprised and also pleased her.

Her brain was a jumble of chaotic thoughts, as were her emotions, though soon one began to take precedence over all the others, arousing a response in her that she did not want to give yet was unable to withhold.

The noise of a hooter finally made him release her. 'You see,' he said shakily, keeping a tight hold of her hand as he stepped back, 'cold water isn't the answer.'

'It's the only one I'm willing to give.'

He began to walk with her, back to where he had parked the car. He did not speak again, but his hand remained clasping hers, warm and strong.

'Is it because you disapprove of my relationship with Dina?' he picked up the thread of their conversation again as he started up the engine.

Kate shrugged. 'Who am I to moralise?'

'Then why do you keep turning me down, when you so obviously fancy me?'

'I don't go in for casual affairs.'

'Why should our affair be casual? I find you extraordinarily exciting.'

'I'm sure you're used to exciting women,' she said drily.

'I'm used to obvious ones.' Scott slowed down to consult a signpost. 'You'd be amazed how few genuinely exciting women there are.'

She found that hard to believe, and though she did not say so, her silence said it for her.

He threw her a sardonic look. 'You think I'm lying, don't you? You have a specific image of me and you're determined not to let anything distort your distortion!'

Kate had to smile. It was difficult to disagree with him when he read her mind so accurately.

'To revert to your previous remark,' he continued, 'how do you know I'm not serious about you?'

His pretence—for that was all it could be—irritated her, and to pay him back, she decided to call his bluff. 'Are you?' she asked sweetly.

Once again he slowed down almost to a stop, but this time it was to look at her.

'That remark of yours, Kate is what's known as taking the bull by the horns.'

'And no doubt makes you feel like a matador who's lost his cape?' she added drily.

'The analogy is certainly apt,' he admitted.

'Then I'll let you off the horns of your dilemma! You needn't bother to answer my question.'

'Don't you want to know the answer?'

'Not particularly.'

'Why, do you think I'd lie to you?'

'If you thought by doing so you'd get what you want—yes,' she replied.

'Then you'd be wrong! I never lie to my girl-friends, and never make promises I know I'm not going to keep.'

'What sort of promises *do* you make?'

'You certainly enjoy putting me on the spot, don't you?' he chuckled goodhumouredly.

'If you remember, from the first I warned you I believed in honesty.'

'How could I forget? It's turned me off cod for life!'

'The idea was to turn you off me for life!' she joked.

This time Scott did stop the car, and he switched off the engine too, so that he could give her his undivided attention. '*Nothing could do that*,' he said fiercely. 'I want you, Kate, more than I've ever wanted any other woman.'

Momentarily, fear gripped her. If he wanted her enough, he could take her and there would be little she could do about it, here amidst the quiet countryside where only the sounds of nature broke the silence. But then rationality returned. Perhaps it was a subconscious wish on her part; a desire for fulfilment without blame. Certainly, Scott was not the type of man who would ever take a woman by force.

'I can't think why,' she answered lightly. 'And I'm not looking for compliments, merely being truthful. What's so special about me?'

'If I could define that, I'd be halfway home to defining why I've been behaving like an adolescent schoolkid ever since the first time we met. I haven't begged for any girl's favour since I was thirteen years old.'

Hope ran high in her, and her heart began to beat so wildly, she could barely form the words. 'Perhaps—perhaps you've fallen in love with me?' she suggested daringly.

If she had expected an admission, she was immediately disappointed. 'Would it make any difference to you if I said I had?'

The lie came more easily than she had expected. 'Of course not,' she answered quickly. 'As I'm not in love with you, how could it?'

'That's what I thought,' he said flatly, and immediately started up the motor.

The abruptness of his change of mood puzzled Kate for the remainder of the day. Although he was attentive, amusing, even teasing, it was in a distracted sort of way, as if his mind were somewhere else—perhaps on someone or something else. In fact she would not have been surprised if he had suggested returning to Dublin after lunch. But instead they toured Wicklow, and even went for a walk on the beach at Brittas Bay, the golden sands completely deserted except for one man and his dog.

'The sea may look like the Mediterranean,' said Kate, bending down to test the temperature, 'but it certainly doesn't feel like it!'

'And I was hoping you'd be tempted to skinny-dip!' Scott looked crestfallen.

With a flourish she produced two tiny wisps of silk from her handbag. 'Once a Girl Guide, always a Girl Guide!' she smiled.

'For the cover that bikini would provide, you might as well have skinny-dipped!' he responded. 'I hope your Guides training has prepared you for other temptations too—such as nightdress and toothbrush!'

'How very old-fashioned of you, Scott,' she said, her green eyes wide. 'To be prepared for *that*, I'd only need a toothbrush!'

'You're never short of an answer, are you?' he smiled.

'Not when the questions are such obvious ones!'

He chuckled. 'I led with the chin on that one.'

'No more than usual.'

'I guess that's true. I like to see the sparks shooting from your green eyes. And they're genuinely green, Kate, no hazel nonsense about them. You must have Irish blood somewhere.'

'Perhaps we both have,' she suggested. 'You've more than a touch of the blarney yourself!'

'Judging by my failure with you, my "touch" must be deserting me!'

'Don't dwell on it unduly,' she smiled. 'You're the last in a long line!'

'Care to give me any hints on how the others succeeded?' he questioned.

'They didn't,' she said in honeyed tones. 'I'm frigid by nature.'

'Like hell you are. You may defrost slowly, but your kisses could melt an iceberg.'

'Don't read too much into *that*!'

Resolutely Kate resumed walking and he kept pace with her. He did not reply to her comment, and they continued in silence, until they reached the end of the beach.

'I wonder what it's like here in high season,' he said, as they turned back and headed for the car.

'As there aren't any hotels here, I can't imagine it being terribly crowded. I believe that's true of most of Ireland. They've kept the coastline quite unspoiled.'

'I hope they continue to do so. I'd hate to think of bodies jammed in like sardines here as they are in the South of France.'

'You must be thinking of Cannes,' Kate smiled. 'The only time I ever sat on the Carlton beach, I was frightened to move in case I poked someone's eye out!'

'Have you done much travelling?' he asked conversationally.

'I've "done" Europe, as you Americans say, or at least most of it, and visited the States twice.'

It was a good neutral topic of conversation, and they explored it in depth over dinner, eaten early because they wanted to get back in time to watch the show live at the TV studios.

Unlike many businessmen who flitted from country to country, Scott made a point of getting to know them—and not just in a touristy way, visiting all the high-spots in air-conditioned coaches and cars.

'As I told you, I rarely take time off just to laze around,' he said, over coffee. 'But I do enjoy exploring.'

'Isn't it rather dangerous to wander off on your own?' she asked, thinking of some of the places he had mentioned.

'That just adds spice to the enjoyment!' He half smiled. 'I suppose, to be really successful, one has to take risks, and I guess it's a trait that spills over into my leisure activities as well.'

'You should have gone into politics,' Kate told him. 'That's full of risks.'

'I pride myself on my honesty in my climb to the top. I'm afraid that's a virtue politicians can never claim.'

'How cynical you are! Surely there must be some honest politicians?' She smiled teasingly. 'How about George Washington?'

'I should have known you'd get the better of me,' he chuckled, and motioned the waiter for the bill.

Scott decided to return to Dublin on the main road. It was now dark, and their previous route might be difficult to follow. In any case, it was far quicker, the owner of the restaurant informed them, when his advice had been sought.

But finding the main road proved more difficult than Scott had imagined, in spite of explicit directions, and before long they were hopelessly lost. Not only that, it had started to drizzle, and there was an ominous rattle emanating from beneath the bonnet of the car, that culminated in it grinding to a complete stop mid-way up a hill.

'Damn!' Scott swore under his breath. 'I'm a man of many talents, but the inside of a car is a complete puzzle to me.'

'I'm afraid I'm not much better,' said Kate. 'But open the bonnet anyway, just in case it's only a loose wire or the fan-belt. There's probably a spare in the tool kit.'

'Even if there is, I don't suppose I'll be able to change it,' he grumbled.

'It might tell you how to in the manual, but if not, it's probably just a case of undoing a few screws,' Kate volunteered practically.

'An optimist, I see,' he commented dryly, but nevertheless he stepped out, and using a torch he had found in the boot, scrutinised the inside of the bonnet.

'As far as I can tell, it isn't a loose wire or the fan-belt,' he shouted after a few minutes.

'Then close the bonnet and come back in the car,' she called back. 'There's no point in standing out there and getting soaked!'

'BMWs never break down,' he said, angrily mopping his wet brow and greasy hands with a handkerchief.

'They do when someone's tampered with them.' Kate voiced the thought that had occurred to her immediately, but had kept to herself, giving him the benefit of her doubt, in the hope that he could rectify the fault.

'And what's *that* supposed to mean?' he questioned belligerently.

'I'm sure you don't need an explanation,' she said in honeyed tones.

'If you mean what I think you mean—'

'I do,' she cut in calmly, amazed at her self-control.

Scott ran a hand through his hair, a particular habit of his in times of stress.

'I may have chased you like a lovesick kid, because I'm crazy about you, but that doesn't mean I've completely lost my marbles!'

But Kate did not believe him. Her refusal to give in to him had turned his conquering instinct into an obsession; had made him so determined to have his way that he no longer cared how he achieved it. Well, if he thought she was going to spend the night with him in the car—where she knew the seats conveniently converted into a bed— then he had another think coming!

'I'm not some sex-starved young pup who needs to trick a girl into spending the night with him,' Scott continued angrily. 'If all I wanted was to go to bed with you, I'd have made sure it was somewhere a darned sight more comfortable than this car!'

'Knowing how thorough you are, I'm sure there's an excellent four-star hotel within walking distance,' she retorted.

He leaned over and opened the door. 'Then I suggest you get out and find it.'

One look at his grim countenance told her that he meant it, and obstinately refusing to retract, in spite of the downpour in progress, Kate stepped out of the car.

She was soaked before she had gone ten yards, and frightened too, with only the glow of the car's headlights and rear lights to give any comfort, but unless she wanted to walk backwards, there was no way she could keep them constantly in sight. In any case, the road curved, and then it was total darkness.

Silently she cursed the Irish weather, though the rain was no different from any other. The only difference was that she was walking in it out of pigheadedness, not necessity. She knew she could not go on for much longer, not because her clothes were wet, nor her hair plastered to her head and face, where the wind had whipped it. It was sheer funk. If only Scott were here, at least that would be some solace. She would even be willing to apologise, for having reached the brow of the hill, she could see, even in the dark, that the only light for miles around came from a tiny cottage some half a mile away.

Well, to compensate for the unjustness of her accusations, she would return to the car, and tell him. Perhaps he would then walk to the cottage and telephone for a taxi. No, she amended hastily—they would both walk to the cottage. She did not fancy being alone in the car for any length of time.

But there was no need to go back, for at that moment she heard a chuckle, and then Scott was beside her, holding a large umbrella over her head.

Immediately she forgot her good intentions and rounded on him furiously.

'Do you mean to say you allowed me to walk all this way on my own without an umbrella, while—'

'But you weren't alone. I've been behind you all the way. I'm too much of a gentleman to allow a lady to walk unaccompanied on a deserted country lane. Think what could happen to her!'

Even in the dark Kate was aware of the amused quirk that lifted one corner of his mouth and could sense, even though she could not see, the glint in his eye.

'Nothing as bad as what's going to happen to you!' she snapped angrily. 'Of all the selfish, cruel, inconsiderate—'

He caught hold of her two hands as she pummelled at his chest, almost dropping the umbrella in stopping her.

'I just wanted to teach you a lesson,' he said, surprisingly gently, 'and a little water never harmed anyone. Perhaps now you'll stop jumping to conclusions about me!'

It was pointless to stand arguing in the rain, and they both realised it. Scott took her arm in his and they half walked, half ran to the cottage.

'Car broken down, has it?' The burly, weatherbeaten man who answered their knock quickly summed up their predicament. 'Come inside and dry yourselves off by the fire. You look half drowned, missus.'

Introducing himself as Liam Murphy, he immediately busied himself with the kettle, and within five minutes had brewed a pot of tea, which he poured into three large, thick mugs.

'I'm afraid you'll have to stay here till morning when the bus comes by. I don't have a car or a telephone—and the nearest box is a couple of miles away. Not that it would be of much use,' he added. 'There's no garage open this time of night anyway.'

'What about a taxi?' Scott suggested. 'I wouldn't mind walking to the box if I could get one.'

'There's nothing locally, and I doubt if anyone would come down from Dublin on a night like this.'

It was not always possible to follow the old man's conversation, for he had a heavy brogue, and on several occasions Scott had to apologise, and ask him to repeat himself. He did so goodnaturedly, telling them he lived alone, and that, until his retirement, had been a farm hand. Now he kept a few animals himself, and with his pension, managed to eke out a living.

'Well, missus, you look completely done in,' he commented, noticing Kate yawn. 'I've only one bedroom, but you and yer man are welcome to it.'

'We wouldn't dream of turning you out of your bed,' Kate said hastily. 'We'll be quite happy in here, thank you.'

Liam Murphy looked momentarily embarrassed. 'You won't when those little devils decide to wake up,' he said, indicating a box in the corner of the small, low-ceilinged room. 'Their mammy died and I'm rearing them by hand. They'll be all over the place, and unlike Patsy here,' he nodded down at the cross-Collie, sleeping at his feet, 'them little piglets aren't housetrained!'

'In that case we'll accept your kind offer,' Scott interjected promptly. 'Don't worry,' he whispered to Kate when the old man had disappeared to find some clean sheets, 'I'll sleep on the floor with my hands and legs tied, if needs be, but I've no intention of sharing a room with that little lot! You may consider them part of the four-star luxury treatment I had in mind for you, but I'm afraid I don't!'

Kate felt herself redden. 'I apologise for disbelieving you,' she said stiffly.

'I'm used to it by now,' he said wryly. 'But perhaps after tonight, you'll at least *try* to give me the benefit of your doubts!' He rose from his chair and went to stand by the fire. 'Talking of four-star luxury, I wonder if there are indoor facilities.'

The question was answered by the reappearance of Liam Murphy, who proudly showed them the bathroom he himself had installed. It was little more than a cubbyhole, but it functioned perfectly, and Kate was even able to soak in a bath full of hot water.

Afterwards, she stepped into one of Liam Murphy's capacious flannel nightgowns, as her clothes, including her underwear, were still not sufficiently dry to put back on again, and the blanket she had been draped in was needed for Scott.

'You look like Little Orphan Annie!' Scott smiled, when she joined him in the bedroom.

'You don't exactly look a picture of sartorial elegance yourself!' she retorted, eyeing the grey blanket, draped around his large frame like a toga, the length mid-thigh on him, whereas on her it had reached the ground.

'I'm perfectly willing to divest, if you prefer!' he grinned wickedly. 'I usually sleep in the buff anyway.'

'I thought you promised to behave yourself,' Kate smiled.

'That's exactly what I thought I was doing,' he proclaimed indignantly. 'Otherwise I wouldn't have bothered to ask your permission to divest!'

'That chair doesn't look very comfortable.' Kate decided a change of subject was called for, though in the intimacy of the small room it was not going to be easy to keep away from the subject of bed, at least until they had settled who was going to sleep where.

'I'll manage,' Scott responded. 'Naturally, you'll take the bed.'

It was a large brass one, and though the sheets were of the cheapest material, they were spotlessly clean, as was the rest of the house, in spite of the fact Liam Murphy was a bachelor, and allowed farmyard animals to wander around at will.

Feeling dreadfully guilty—the bed, which had probably belonged to Liam's parents, was easily wide enough to accommodate the two of them—Kate snuggled beneath the covers, and watched with some amusement as Scott tried to manoeuvre his six feet two inch frame into a comfortable position in the narrow, upright armchair.

'"It is a far, far better thing that I do, than I have ever done,"' Scott quoted Sydney Carton's immortal line as he went to the guillotine, in *A Tale of Two Cities*. 'And I hope you darn well appreciate it!'

Kate giggled, and blew him a kiss, before turning off the bedside light. 'You'll never know how much!'

With only the steady ticking of the clock on the pine chest of drawers to disturb the peace, Kate fell asleep in moments, but was surprised to find, when she awoke, that it was still dark. Because she did not want to disturb Scott, she was reluctant to put on the light to find out the exact time, and it was not until she heard the grandfather clock in the kitchen chime that she realised it was only three o'clock.

'Are you awake?' she whispered, as she heard a rustle on the other side of the room.

'I haven't been to sleep yet,' Scott answered. 'I'm afraid, apart from not being a very good mechanic, I've discovered I'm not a very good contortionist either!'

Kate began to feel even guiltier. What harm would there be in allowing him to sleep on the bed?

'*On* as against in,' she emphasised, when she finally put thought to words, adding: 'And make sure you keep your distance.'

'I told you earlier on you were safe with me, although I'm not going to pretend I don't want you. Any more than I'm going to go on pretending the reason I can't sleep has anything to do with this chair. I could sleep standing up.'

Something in his voice warned her of a change of mood. It was no longer light and teasing, and if she had not known better, she would have thought he had been drinking, for his words ran into each other, as if he had little or no control over them.

He padded across the stone floor and came to stand by the bed. 'Do you mind if I switch on the light? I have something to say, and I'd like to see, even if I can't touch!' He did not wait for her to reply, but bent down and pressed the switch on the bedside lamp. His wide shoulders blocked most of the glow, but his agitation was clearly discernible, his eyes glittering, his mouth tightly set.

'Haven't you realised yet that it's not just a bedroom relationship I have in mind for us?' he said.

Kate sat up, and forced herself to look directly at him. She was not certain what he was trying to say to her, and after the disappointment of the afternoon, when she had suspected he might be about to tell her he loved her, she was frightened to allow herself to hope again.

'Why *should* I have realised it?' she demanded coolly.

'Because I've made a complete fool of myself over you.' There was frustration in his voice. 'Don't you know I haven't been able to get you out of my mind since I met you?'

'You've certainly been persistent.' She made herself sound casual. 'But then you're not the sort of man who gives up easily on anything.'

'But that's exactly it,' he stated forcefully. 'As far as women are concerned, one rejection's usually enough. I've never had to beg for their favour, and if that sounds conceited, it wasn't meant to. It's just that I've never really cared what girl I was with, as long as she was good in bed, and pretty to look at.' His voice was husky, no doubt caused through lack of sleep. 'At least that's how it was until you.'

Suddenly Kate's heart began to pound, and she was glad she was lying down. *Had* she misread his intentions all along? Was it possible she really meant something to him?

'I did everything but fall down on my knees to get *you* to come out with me,' he went on, 'and even when I finally succeeded, it was only after I'd ordered you to, and used the pretext of a business discussion.' His mouth curled in remembrance. 'It didn't do much for my ego, I can tell you!'

'I'm sure it was big enough to take it!' she commented drily. 'And you guessed I wasn't fooled—you even said as much.'

'I know, but then when you walked out on me, and refused to listen when I came down to see you at your parents' . . . Well, I thought perhaps you weren't just annoyed with me because of my behaviour with Dina, but didn't give a damn for me.'

'Why are you telling me this now?'

He did not flinch from the question, but met her gaze full on. 'Because I can't bear to go on having you so near and yet so far away from me. I have to know if you care a little for me . . . if I stand any kind of chance. Do I, Kate?' he asked softly. 'Do I?'

Although she longed to reveal her own feelings, she still held back.

'What about Dina?' she asked.

'Whatever my relationship with her, you have my word I've never loved her, and for the past few months she's been strictly a business proposition—I thought I'd made that clear by chasing after you.'

'I was so blinded by jealousy, I didn't believe you,' she whispered. 'Just as I didn't believe you tonight when the car broke down.'

'Does that mean you believe me now?' he questioned eagerly.

'Yes,' she answered simply. 'Yes, Scott, it does.'

'And that you do have some feeling for me?'

'Some?' she repeated, her heart in her eyes. 'I love you. Haven't you realised that yet?'

With a groan he leaned over to kiss her, soft, tender kisses all over her face, before he came to her lips. Even then passion did not appear, and she was touched at his restraint.

'Holding you like this, and knowing you love me, is like a dream come true,' he said huskily. 'The number of times I've longed to tell you how I felt, but didn't dare. Even this afternoon, I couldn't find the courage.'

'I was just as frightened,' she confessed shyly. 'I thought if you knew . . . you might take advantage of it.'

'What makes you think I won't now?' he questioned, cupping her face in his hands.

'I don't.' She twined her fingers through his thick hair. 'But now it doesn't matter.'

'Do you really mean that?' Scott asked jerkily.

For answer, she pushed back the covers and reached for the light switch.

Once more he kissed her, and knowing herself loved and not just desired, she unashamedly let him see how much she needed him, nestling close and loosening the knot of his blanket, to stroke his shoulders and run her hands down his back.

The feathery movement of her fingers was his final undoing, and he parted her lips in a kiss of tantalising intimacy. With practised ease he undid the buttons of her nightgown, and slipped her free, then pressed the whole length of his body against hers. His hands were warm on her, moving lightly up and down, exploring, touching, rubbing, bringing her to a pitch of longing she had never before known.

Hesitantly, at first, and then gaining in confidence as her passion heightened, Kate met like with like, stroking his wildly throbbing body until she began to know each bone, each muscle, each indentation, as well as she knew each feature of his beloved face.

'I've wanted this for so long. I love you, Kate,' he muttered thickly. 'I love you more than life itself.'

Again he claimed her lips, again he caressed, again he teased, tantalised, aroused, until for both of them only the ultimate act of love would satisfy.

Receptive as she was, she was prepared for pain, but his skill in bringing her within a hairsbreadth of fulfilment in the moments preceding ensured that it was minimal, and only a slight, constrictive movement betrayed her.

'Darling, adorable, sweetest Kate,' he murmured. 'I never guessed . . . Are you sure this is what you really want?'

'I'm very sure, Scott,' she whispered, loving him all the more for his willingness to draw back.

Then time seemed to be suspended. No longer were they two different people, but two halves of a whole, carried away on a wave of passion that grew more and more tumultuous with each thrust, until finally the floodgates of desire opened and burst into a rapturous, quivering climax.

It was some time before either of them spoke, and then it was only to murmur the sweet nothings and endearments that passed for conversation in the aftermath of lovemaking. They were content to lie quietly in each other's arms, savouring the languor of their perfect union; made even more perfect for Kate because Scott had finally said that he loved her. Although the words had been uttered at the height of passion, she hugged them to her, knowing he had meant them.

She must have fallen asleep, for the next thing she was aware of was the sun streaming through the half-open floral curtains, and a cup of tea resting on the bedside table.

Of Scott there was no sign, only the imprint of his body on the bed and pillow. Lazily she stretched. Unlike romantic fiction, morning light had not brought pangs of guilt, only a feeling of contentment that they had a future together. His unburdening last night clearly showed he needed her as much as he wanted her. For how long she did not know, nor would she press for a commitment. The fact that they had some kind of future together was all that mattered for the moment. Kate smiled to herself. How quickly she had changed her mind! Only a short while ago she had refused to contemplate an affair. But now she knew Scott loved her, she was willing to take him on any terms.

A few minutes later the man in her thoughts entered the room, and fixed her with a look that was both tender and affectionate.

'I woke early, and had breakfast with Liam before he left for work,' Scott said, kissing her gently on the top of her tousled head, before seating himself on the bed beside her. 'How's the tea?'

Kate reached for the cup and sipped it appreciatively. 'You make a good strong brew, for an American. Is this the extent of your culinary prowess, or can you cook as well?'

He took the cup from her hand and placed it back on the table, then cupped her chin in his hand and bent down to kiss her full on the lips. It was not a passionate kiss to arouse; loving, rather than lover-like.

'I don't want you to learn *all* my secrets in one go! I'd rather you discovered them a little at the time.'

She read several different meanings into his words, finding consolation in each one.

'Other than your underwear, I'm afraid your things are rather the worse for their soaking,' said Scott, claiming her attention again, as he indicated her crumpled suit lying on the armchair. 'As it's my fault, let me buy you a new one. I've been told the best shops here are in Grafton Street. We'll drive straight there and replace it.'

'I wouldn't dream of it,' Kate protested. 'I've had it ages anyway.' It was a lie, as she had bought it just before leaving London, and paid the earth for it too. But she found the idea of him buying clothes for her embarrassing, while at the same time appreciating that after last night's intimacy and promise, she was acting rather naïvely.

He looked as if he were about to argue, but then thought better of it. 'In spite of last night, you're still my sweet, innocent little Kate,' he teased fondly. 'And I hope you always will be. It's one of the things I like best about you.'

'You can tell me all the other things you like about me when I'm dressed!' she smiled, then added: 'I hope you realise we're both in for it, for missing the chat show last night?'

'Lord!' he swore softly. 'I'd not given it a thought. But don't worry, I'll handle Dina.'

'Are you going to tell her the truth?' she asked, trying to sound casual.

'Would you like me to tell her the *whole* truth?' he teased.

Kate felt herself blush. 'I suppose not.'

He smiled, and walked over to the door. 'There's a bus every hour—that gives you twenty minutes.'

She was ready in less, but she needn't have bothered to

rush, as the bus was late. The nearest village was only four stops away, and Scott headed straight for the garage. After arranging to hire the owner's car, which he promised would be returned by the man sent out by the rental company to collect the BMW, they set off at once for Dublin.

Scott was strangely silent on the journey. Could he be concerned about his explanation to Dina? Somehow she doubted it. Other than as a business investment, she now believed what he had asserted all along—that the actress no longer meant anything to him. Last night had finally convinced her.

CHAPTER NINE

As soon as they arrived back at the hotel, Scott excused himself. He had several phone calls to make, but more urgently wanted to shave and change. Liam had only possessed a cut-throat razor, and he had preferred to wait and use his own electric one.

'I'd like to have spent the day with you,' he told Kate regretfully. 'But I have a luncheon engagement, and it will probably carry over to late afternoon. How about you and Gary joining Dina and me for dinner this evening?'

Surprised, and also disappointed, that he intended for them to carry on as before, Kate declined.

'I don't think it's a very good idea. Whether you tell Miss Dalton the truth about us or not, she'll probably guess we slept together. In her place, I'd jump to the same conclusion.'

'You mean you wouldn't trust me either?' he smiled.

'You said it, not me.'

'You're angry with me, aren't you?' he said, catching hold of her arm, as she turned away from him and headed towards the lifts.

'If you want me to be perfectly honest, then yes, I am angry. I'd thought—'

'You were quite right to think it too,' he said, not allowing her to finish. 'But I can't put Dina out of my life at the moment. You know why, and I had hoped you'd continue to understand.'

'I'm sorry, but I don't.' They were alone in the lift and it had stopped at her floor. 'Perhaps it would be better if I just shook your hand and said it was nice knowing you,' she said flippantly. 'After last night, I certainly do—in the biblical sense at least!'

'Don't be cheap!' he rebuked her sharply. 'You're not like that.'

'You're certainly treating me as if I am!' she snapped, and ran down the corridor to her bedroom.

But she was no match for his long strides, as he came tearing after her.

'You little fool!' he muttered, gripping her shoulder angrily. 'Don't you know how much I care for you? You've no need to be jealous of Dina, or any other woman for that matter—you're the only one I love—have *ever* loved.' His eyes stared directly into hers. The subdued lighting of the hallway had made the pupils dilate and the irises were just a fine gold rim. 'I'm only asking you to play along with me for another week at the most. Then I'll arrange to be called away on business, and won't return. By the time Dina comes back to London, there'll only be a few days' shooting left, and I'll be able to tell her about us.'

'What about your business here? Will that be completed so quickly?' she questioned.

'You're my *only* business here.' His look said it all. 'And I completed it satisfactorily last night!'

'Oh, Scott, I do love you!' She reached up to kiss him, and immediately he drew her close.

'Don't ever stop,' he answered softly, and with his index finger traced the bones of her face; the short straight nose, the high cheekbones, the rounded jawline. 'We have a lot to talk over and plan, but this isn't the time or the place.' He indicated the chambermaid, wheeling a cleaning trolley along the corridor.

Then he was gone, striding to the lift again, not looking

back, as if afraid that if he did he would return and never let her go.

Kate closed her bedroom door and leaned against it. Although she had agreed to give Scott another week with Dina, she was still upset by his request. The thought of the two of them together was more than she could bear—even though he had assured her she had no need to be jealous. If only she could be certain what he had meant by it. She had longed to ask him, but had been frightened of his anger. After all, if she did not trust him now, could there be any hope for their future?

After confirming an interview for Dina with *Irish Tatler* for the following day, Kate had little to occupy her, and she decided to see some of the sights. There was a guided coach tour leaving the hotel after lunch, and she booked a seat on it.

The weather brightened up sufficiently for Dublin to be seen at its best, and she particularly enjoyed the drive along the Liffey Quais to Phoenix Park, and the State Apartments in Dublin Castle.

When she saw Gary in the bar before dinner, he accepted her explanation of the car's breakdown, and the subsequent events, with cynical good-humour, barely raising an eyebrow when she assured him that Scott had behaved like a perfect gentleman.

'I only hope Miss Dalton believed it too,' Kate added.

'*Honi soit qui mal y pense*,' Gary quoted with a grin. 'Anyway, you won't have long to wait to find out—here she is.'

The bar was fairly full, and everyone turned to watch the actress's progress.

'I hope I'm not disturbing you two?' Dina beamed to Gary, including Kate in it as if by second thought. 'Scott had a call from London that looks as if it's going to go on for ages, so I thought I'd wander down without him.'

'Have a drink with us—we're on champagne,' Gary indicated the bottle of Moët et Chandon in the ice bucket. 'But if you'd like something else . . .'

'That's fine for me too.'

He beckoned the waiter to bring another glass, and while they waited, Kate noticed Dina twisting an exquisite diamond and sapphire bracelet on her wrist. It matched her earrings, and the pendant round her throat.

'Lovely, isn't it?' she asked, aware of Kate's gaze. 'Scott gave it to me only an hour ago. As *you* know, he's been a naughty boy, and I guess this is his way of saying sorry.'

Jealousy seared Kate like a red-hot poker. No doubt this was the reason Scott had been unable to spend any time with her today. Finding a suitable present to appease Dina had been far more important to him.

'A very naughty boy, if price is anything to go by,' Gary chimed in mischievously. 'They're a hundred thousand dollars' worth if they're a cent!'

'Only he and Kate know the answer to *that*,' Dina said dulcetly. 'But I'm not one to hold a grudge, as long as I get what I want in the end.'

Did she mean Scott? Kate wondered. It was obvious the girl suspected they had slept together, yet was willing to forgive. But then why shouldn't she? From her point of view, marriage to Scott had everything to commend it; money and power, to further her career, as well as an attractive and dynamic escort. His wandering eye might even prove an asset—what was sauce for the goose was, after all, sauce for the gander, Kate remembered the passionate love scene she had watched Dina perform with her leading man. Perhaps it had not been just another indication of her acting ability, as Kate had assumed, but for real.

The appearance of Scott saved her from further unsavoury speculation. He came striding into the bar, looking neither to left nor right.

'I have to fly back to London tonight,' he announced without preamble. 'And I'm taking Kate with me. How soon can you be ready?' he asked, looking at her, but not meeting her eyes.

His request surprised her, as did his brusque manner. 'Is anything wrong?' she asked.

'Yes. But it's a business matter—to do with the hotel,' he explained, addressing Gary and Dina. 'I'd rather discuss it when we're alone.'

'How long will you be gone?' Dina asked.

He shrugged. 'As long as it takes to clear up the mess. But Kate won't be returning anyway, so you'll have to manage without her.' He bent down to kiss her cheek. 'Don't bother to see me off. Stay here with Gary, and have dinner.'

'I'll phone you as soon as I get back to London,' Gary told Kate.

Before she could reply, Scott caught her by the arm and steered her towards the exit.

He refused to answer any of her questions until they reached her room, and as soon as they stepped inside he pushed her on to the bed, and faced her belligerently.

'Your boy-friend's escaped with the money,' he said, his voice flat, but his eyes sparkling with fury. 'Mike Wentworth is now somewhere in South America—although no doubt *you* know exactly where, and will be going to join him.'

For a brief instant Kate tried to pretend he had not spoken, and that her imagination was playing a trick on her. But as she went on staring into Scott's face, she knew she had heard correctly.

'Well?' he demanded. 'Haven't you anything to say?'

'What *can* I say—except that it's as much a shock to me as it is to you.'

He watched her for a moment without speaking. 'My God, you're a better actress than Dina! If I didn't know better, I'd swear you were telling the truth.'

'But I *am*,' she insisted. 'How can you believe anything else?'

'Because there's no way he could have discovered we were on to him unless he got a look at those documents in your safe.' Scott's voice was grim. 'You're the only other person with a key to it, besides myself.'

His accusation brought Kate to her feet. 'What about *your* safe?' she contended. 'You have a duplicate copy.'

'The same applies. Other than myself, only Hal has a key—and he's the last person I'd ever suspect of cheating me.'

'You'd rather suspect me!' she cried.

'It all fits, doesn't it?' He spat out the words as if he wanted to hit her with each one. 'You knew from reading the documents that his arrest was imminent, but couldn't be made in my absence. Perhaps you thought by sleeping with me you'd be able to persuade me to drop the charges. Well, fortunately for him, he decided not to rely on your charms, but his own instinct.'

Now Kate understood why Mike had always managed to live so well. What an idiot she had been to believe he could have done so by buying and selling shares! With his extravagant tastes and habits, even his high salary would have left little over to invest.

'I see you're not bothering to deny it any more,' Scott said curtly, mistaking her silence for agreement. 'I've met some two-timing bitches in my life, but you're in a class of your own!'

Kate turned away from him, afraid that if she went on looking at him she would break down. Whatever there had been between them was finished. Even when he discovered the truth about her, she would never have anything further to do with him. What chance of happiness could there ever be for them, if he believed her capable of such duplicity?

'When I think of the way you pulled the wool over my eyes, I could strangle you—playing hard to get to keep my interest going, and then last night playing the little innocent—pretending it was the first time for you!'

If he could think that of her, there was nothing more to say. 'We aren't going to serve any purpose standing here arguing,' she said wearily. 'If you'll leave me alone, I'll pack. Am I going to be arrested when I get back? If so, I'll telephone my parents and ask them to arrange for a lawyer to be present.'

'Arrested?' he echoed, and pulled her round to face him. 'I despise you for what you've done, but it wasn't for your own gain—just some kind of misguided loyalty to the man you're obviously besotted with.' He peered into her face, as if he could barely see her. 'No one but ourselves will ever know the part you've played. I could never—'

'Spare me your charity. Keep it for some more deserving cause,' Kate cut in scornfully, wrenching herself from his hold. 'I intend to prove my innocence if it takes every penny I've got—but whatever the outcome, after today you'll never see me again.'

The flight back to London was accomplished in almost total silence, and she refused his offer of a lift as they came out of Customs. When they reached the exit, she did not bother to say goodbye, and wheeled her trolley towards the taxi rank without so much as a backward glance.

With the financial aid of her parents, the first thing Kate did was to employ a good firm of private detectives. She was convinced that if Mike could be traced, he would completely clear her name, and would no doubt be horrified to discover she had been implicated in any way.

Finding him was a slow process, though Bill Thomas, the agency's most experienced man, closely questioned his accomplices—bar staff and waiters in the main, who were out on bail pending trial—as well as his friends.

'I agree with Mr Jeffreys,' Bill Thomas told her. 'There is only one way Mr Wentworth could have got into your safe, and that's with the key. But if you say you kept it on you at all times . . .'

The mystery of Mike's whereabouts was finally solved when the detective discovered a love-nest in Fulham, where he had kept a mistress for the past year. Kate was not at all surprised at the revelation, but still believed that whatever else Mike had done, he had not lied about his feelings towards her. But she had not been sleeping with him, and had certainly not expected him to lead the life of a celibate during the period of their association.

'I have a complete sworn statement, witnessed by a reputable lawyer,' Bill Thomas informed her by telephone from Salvador in Brazil, two days after he had flown there to confront Mike. 'Naturally, Mr Wentworth completely exonerates you. Apparently he managed to get hold of your key when you left your handbag on his desk, and then were called away for several minutes. He took an impression with some locksmith's putty he'd been carrying around with him for weeks, hoping a chance would occur.'

Kate immediately forwarded a photostatted copy of the statement to Scott, but did not include a note. His reply, which came by hand on the same day he heard from her, was short, but eloquent.

'What can I say—other than forgive me.'

That evening he telephoned, and though she refused to speak to him, he went on telephoning and writing every day for the next three months. She returned his letters unopened, and if she was unfortunate enough to answer any of his calls, immediately put down the receiver.

He had not lied about ending his association with Dina. By the time the actress returned to the States at the end of July, her name was being romantically linked with her co-star, Bruce Raymonde.

When Kate thought about Scott, which she did far too often for her own peace of mind, she accepted that he had been honest with her all along. She had refused to believe him only because she herself saw relationships in black and white. Using someone for expediency, as he had used Dina—and very probably vice versa—was something that was not in her nature to understand, and had constantly confused her.

The one person Kate had not expected to hear from again was Mike, but he wrote her a long letter, apologising for all the trouble and expense he had caused her, and offering to reimburse her expenses. As the money he wanted to repay did not belong to him, acceptance was out of the question. But at least it showed a certain sense of decency. He also told her that he had bought a partnership in a small hotel, and was hoping to build it up into something bigger and better.

Her own future, though, was of rather more interest to her, and in spite of parental objections—they thought she should take a holiday first—she started to look for premises for the Public Relations company she intended to start with her friend from Granada Television.

Within a month she had leased a small office in a block in Sloane Street. The rental was high, considering the square footage involved, but both Kate and her friend Wendy felt that a good address was essential.

Clients proved to be no problem. Wendy's contacts were numerous and influential, as were her own, and by Christmas, they were earning more than in their old jobs. Money, although nice to have, was not the motivating factor for either of them, any more than it had been previously. They both enjoyed their complete independence, as well as the reputation they were establishing.

'I see Scott Jeffreys is in the news again,' Wendy remarked, a week prior to the holidays, handing Kate the *Daily Telegraph*, open at the financial page. 'He's building a new hotel overlooking Hyde Park, and apparently has decided to leave Blakes more or less as it is, and run it as an entirely individual entity.'

Kate showed her surprise. 'I'm sure Mr Blake will be delighted to hear it.'

'It's amazing to think he got permission to build on this particular piece of land,' Wendy went on. 'At least half a dozen other developers have been turned down.'

'Scott was never one to take no for an answer,' Kate stated flatly, as she glanced down at the newspaper. There was a small picture of him at the head of the article, and the attractively craggy features brought back memories she would rather have forgotten.

The London Midas would be completed by the following December, she read, and would follow the design of all the other hotels in the group. When asked if he regretted buying Blakes, in view of his latest acquisition, Scott had answered that Blakes would always have a special place in his heart.

'Should I ever decide to sell my company, I'll still retain my interest in it, and run it as a hobby.'

'I wonder what brought about his change of heart,' Kate commented.

'Perhaps you did,' Wendy suggested.

Kate made a disclaiming gesture. 'I'm sure *my* opinion wouldn't influence him. I doubt if he ever gives me a thought now.' Wendy and Lucy were the only two of her friends who knew the true story of her sudden leavetaking. Everyone else had been told she had walked out after another stormy scene with Dina Dalton, and because they knew her association with the actress had not been a happy one, her lie had been accepted without question. 'I read in one of the gossip columns that he's been squiring Ann Morrissey around.' Kate named an American socialite. 'Perhaps he's hoping to impress her. I believe she's some kind of preservation nut.'

'Didn't she once chain herself to the railings of some hideous old building in a New York slum?'

Kate nodded. 'And because she's Ann Morrissey, they didn't knock it down—or at least not until the following year, when she was busy giving her all to some other worthy cause!'

'Miaow, *miaow*!'

'Okay, so I'm jealous,' Kate admitted goodhumouredly. 'But can I help it if I still love the guy?'

'Then why the hell don't you do something about it?'

'Such as?'

'Go and see him. He couldn't have done more to try to get you back.'

'If he'd really loved me, he would never have thought so badly of me,' Kate argued stubbornly.

'He didn't accuse *you* of stealing the money, darling. He just thought you were so in love with Mike you were willing to tell him he was under suspicion, so he could get away. And if you could look at it unbiasedly, the facts did add up. So what else could he think?'

'He didn't love me enough to trust me,' Kate said doggedly. 'And if he didn't then, he never will.'

The finality of her tone told her friend that she did not want to discuss the matter any further.

'Why don't you spend part of the holidays in the sun?' Wendy suggested, taking the hint and changing the subject. 'Ten whole days with your parents is a bit of a bore, surely?'

'Only because they'll be busy most of the time. The hotel's completely full and they're always short-staffed over Christmas. I've promised to lend a hand, in fact.'

'You're crazy,' her friend said. 'You've been working a six-day week since we started, and your social life is almost non-existent. Why don't you go somewhere in the sun, where you'll meet people?'

'You mean men, don't you?' said Kate with amusement.

'What's wrong with men? Or are you planning to be an old maid?'

Wendy was right, of course. It was about time she put Scott behind her, and gave some thought to her future; a future she had no intention of spending alone.

'I could leave the day after Boxing Day,' Kate said. 'But then I'll have barely a week until we open up the office again.'

'What's the point in being your own boss if you can't take some extra time off?' Wendy smiled. 'I can easily manage, especially as we've got that secretary starting on January the first.'

A sizeable cheque, promised by her parents for a Christmas present, meant that within reason, money was no problem, and for a couple of days Kate pored over the travel brochures. Florida was out of the question, in spite of guaranteed sunshine—it was Scott's home base, and although the chances of running into him were a million to one, the odds were still too high for her to take a chance. Finally, heeding the advice of several friends, she plumped for Hawaii.

'Have you any particular hotel in mind?' the girl in the travel agency asked her. 'It's high season, and you've left it for the last moment.'

'Anywhere reasonable, as long as the hotel isn't part of the Midas group,' Kate replied.

With several of the outfits she had bought for her trip to Ireland still unworn, she only needed to top up on beachwear, but wandering around Knightsbridge, it was difficult to resist temptation, and as usual, she ended up with far more than she would probably wear.

She decided to have her hair restyled too, going to a hairdresser who, although the darling of the smart set, did not just follow current trends, but studied your face to make sure they suited you.

'This fringe is far too heavy for a dainty little thing like you,' he said, as he sent to work with his scissors, shaping and layering, before finally finger-drying it. 'Much better for the hair,' he assured her, 'and with this style you really don't need a dryer. Give yourself time to get used to your new look,' he instructed. 'I'm sure when you do you'll never want to go back to the old one.'

Studying her reflection in the mirror, Kate conceded that he was probably right. She looked like a sophisticated urchin, and though the cut was almost masculine in length, it did not detract from her femininity, but served to highlight it even more. Copper-coloured fronds curved forward on to her forehead and the hollows of her cheeks, while more tendrils caressed the lobes of her ears but left her neck free to rise, white and slender from the collar of her dress.

'I've always thought of you as Little Red Riding Hood,' Wendy smiled her approval when she returned to the office. 'But now you'll really have to beat the *wolves* from your door!'

On Christmas Eve Kate drove down to her parents', and because they had such a busy day ahead of them, and would not have time to relax and enjoy their own Christmas lunch, they had roast turkey and all the trimmings that evening.

Up, and in the kitchen by seven the next morning, Kate, dressed in charcoal grey cashmere sweater and matching grey tweed trousers, helped lay up breakfast trays, and then, at her mother's insistence, relaxed for a few minutes with a cup of coffee and toast.

'I wish you'd have some bacon and eggs as well,' Mrs Ashton said. 'You've lost weight, and it doesn't suit you.'

'Hard work,' Kate lied, and from the disclaiming gesture, knew her mother was not fooled by it. 'Once I'm away, lazing in the sunshine, I'll probably put it all back on again. Now stop nagging,' she smiled, 'and tell me what you want me to do next.'

'Deliver breakfast trays,' her mother answered promptly.

Kate made a face. 'The last time I did it, I caught a couple in an embarrassing position—they'd forgotten to lock the door and put out their "do not disturb" notice.'

'I promise there's no danger of that with Room Thirty,' her mother said firmly, and pointed to a laden tray. 'He's a bachelor, and on his own!'

Kate's knock was promptly answered, and balancing

the tray with practised ease in her left hand, she opened the door and went inside.

'Put it down on the bed,' Scott's voice instructed, as he rose from the armchair by the window and stepped forward to greet her.

Incredulous, she stared at him. He was fully dressed in brown trousers and monogrammed cream silk shirt, open at the neck, and exuded the pleasant scent of either his shampoo, or after-shave.

'Hullo, Kate.'

His voice was deeper than usual; his early morning voice, she recalled, from the night they had spent together in Ireland.

Hastily she blanked out the memory, and placed the tray on the rumpled bed.

'What are you doing here?' she asked coldly, well aware that it had to be with her parents' connivance.

'Don't blame your parents,' he said, immediately understanding her thoughts. 'I bullied and cajoled them until they agreed. I had to see you, and it was the one sure way I had of being alone with you.'

'You could have come to my flat.'

'And have you slam the door in my face?'

She shrugged. 'There's nothing to stop me walking out of here.'

'Somehow I don't think you will,' he said quietly.

She shrugged again. 'If you've taken so much trouble to see me, the least I can do is spare you a few minutes.' She did her best to sound casual. 'We have a reputation for being polite to *all* our guests.'

'Even unwelcome ones.' It was a statement, not a question.

'You said it, not me,' she answered, then went on conversationally. 'I've been keeping track of you in the papers. I was glad to read you've decided not to go ahead with any more alterations to Blakes.'

'I've been keeping track of you too,' he said, ignoring her comment regarding the hotel. 'I know everything about you; what you do, who you see, how well your business is doing—even that you had your hair cut a couple of days ago.' He studied her critically for a moment. 'I like it,' he said, 'although I liked it just as much before.'

Carefully Kate sat on the edge of the bed. Scott regarded her quizzically, then came over to stand directly in front of her.

'You're the least curious girl I've ever known. Aren't you going to ask me *how* I know?' he asked plaintively.

'I'm not particularly interested, but I'm sure you'll tell me anyway.'

'Damn you, Kate Ashton,' he muttered. 'I can see what my life's going to be like with you. Instead of a ring on my finger you'll put one through my nose and lead me by it!'

She stared at him. 'You're not making sense.'

'I stopped making sense the first day I met *you*.' He glanced longingly at the whisky bottle on the bedside table, as if he needed a drink from it to give him courage to continue. 'Don't you realise I've come here because I'm crazy about you?' He groaned, and pulled her up from the bed and into his arms. 'I want you, Kate, more than anything I've ever wanted in my life.'

'I see,' she said, amazed at how cool she sounded, although her heart was pounding so wildly, she imagined it could be heard in the next room. 'And how long will you want me for?'

'A lifetime,' he replied, with such depth that she could not doubt his sincerity. 'Haven't you realised yet that I want to marry you?'

His words gave her such a shock that her legs buckled and she would have fallen had he not been holding her. 'Marry me . . . ? I can't believe it,' she gasped. 'Is this some kind of joke?'

'I guess after the way I behaved in Dublin, I don't deserve you to take me seriously, but if I could only take back what I said to you, I'd—'

She pulled away from him, surprised to find she had the will-power to do so. But she had to sort out her thoughts, and his nearness was making it impossible.

'It's not what you said, it's that you believed it,' she answered.

'I was blinded by jealousy, and wasn't thinking straight. I couldn't bear to think that you loved Mike enough to—'

'After our night together, didn't you realise Mike never meant anything to me?' she cut in, too impatient to allow him to finish. 'Not in the way you did, at least.'

'I wasn't used to handling loving you, so how could I handle trusting you? Remember, Kate darling,' he went on, his voice a thin thread of sound, 'I've always prided myself on being a realist. The only trouble was, I didn't have the sense to recognise a "*real*" woman when I'd found her.'

'Is that why you rushed off to buy that jewellery for Dina—as an insurance policy, in case you changed your mind about me?'

His eyes did not flicker, but regarded her steadily. 'I didn't lie to you about her. The jewellery was a parting gift. When I left you that morning in the hotel, I decided that whatever the consequences, I couldn't go on with Dina as before. To sweeten our parting, I bought her the most expensive suite of jewellery I could find in Dublin. I'd just given it to her, and told her about us, when I received that damn phone call from London, telling me about Mike.'

Kate sighed. 'She made me think it was your way of apologising for being a naughty boy—her words, not mine,' she smiled. 'And I believed her.'

'Dina's a sore loser. I guess she decided to have her revenge by doing a little mix.' For the first time he allowed himself a smile. 'And you always did jump to conclusions about me. But you know I'm not lying now, don't you, Kate?' He came closer. 'Look into my eyes. They'll tell you I'm speaking the truth.'

The tenseness in his voice dared her to refuse him, and she tilted her head to look him fully in the face. Only inches apart, she saw the colour had seeped from his skin and the lines on either side of his mouth were more pronounced than when she had last seen him, six months ago. A muscle in his left cheek was twitching, and incredible though it was, this big, strong, self-assured man was trembling; trembling because he was pleading with her to believe what he said. She continued to stare into his eyes, and seeing the torment in their depths, it was no longer possible to doubt him.

'Dina deserves an Academy Award,' she said drily.

He gave a deep sigh. 'I don't deny I'd toyed with the idea of marrying her—but that was long before I met you, and only because I was tired of playing around.' He sighed again. 'I wanted something good—something that would last. With you I found it, and I never intend to lose it again. You'll never know how much I love you, Kate; your questioning mind . . . your sharp wit . . . the way you argue with me . . .'

'I'd better not start agreeing with you, or you might get bored!'

'There are other things I love about you to compensate,' he said thickly. 'Your big green eyes, that look at me with the innocence of a little girl, your mouth, that kisses with the passion of a woman in love . . .'

'You sound like the hero in a romance,' Kate smiled.

'When I'm with you, I feel like one.'

With a soft cry she took a step forward and moved into the circle of his arms. 'Darling, darling Scott! What a waste these past few months have been when we could have spent them together, like this.'

'I've wasted more time than you.' He rubbed his cheek against her. 'There've been too many girls like Dina in my life, and I'm not proud of it. But from now on there'll only be you.'

She trembled and clung to him. 'I'd rather you didn't make promises for the future. I'm happy to settle for the present.'

'Don't you believe me?'

Afraid to look at him, she buried her head against his shoulder. 'I'm scared to believe you.'

'Then you'll have to travel everywhere with me to make sure,' he smiled. 'Unless you'd rather I sold Midas, and we ran Blakes together?'

'You mean to say you'd do that for me?' Kate asked in wonderment, knowing how proud he was of his business, and how much it meant to him.

Scott nodded. 'I'd do anything to prove how much I care for you. It's taken me a long time to find the girl I want to marry, and I don't intend to be an absentee husband——or father, for that matter,' he added, nuzzling her hair.

His words made her aware of what the future held and she wound her arms around his neck. 'Kiss me, Scott, I've dreamed of this moment for so long.'

With a murmur, he placed his mouth upon hers. His

touch was gentle, but as her lips parted, his kiss deepened, probing the warm moistness.

'Sweet, darling, adorable little Kate,' he whispered, pressing his body tightly against her, his hardness making her aware of how much he wanted her. 'Say you'll marry me at once. I've got a special licence in my pocket, so you've only to name the day. How about the twenty-seventh—or is that too soon?'

'Today would be even better, if it were possible,' she said shakily, and then drew slightly away from him. 'But the twenty-seventh might be rather difficult. I'm flying to Hawaii.'

'You're still flying there,' he smiled, aware she was teasing. 'But not alone, and not in the same hotel. I changed your booking as soon as Wendy told me where you'd decided to go. It's a perfect place for a honeymoon.'

'So she was your spy?'

'Lucy too—they both knew how unhappy you were, and that you were too obstinate to come to me.'

Kate gave a tiny shudder. 'And because of it I might have lost you!'

'Impossible, sweetheart,' he said tenderly, and cupped her chin in his hand. 'Surely you haven't forgotten the secret of my success?'

She smiled, knowing at once. 'You never take no for an answer.'

'Remember that for the next fifty years,' Scott said thickly, and once again moved to claim her lips.

'Will you be tired of me by then?' she asked tremulously.

'Not ever,' he said huskily. *'Not ever.'*

Take these 4 best-selling novels FREE